BOOGEYMAN

BOOGEYMAN

A Novelization by Jeff Mariotte
Screenplay by Eric Kripke and
Juliet Snowden & Stiles White
Story by Eric Kripke

POCKET STAR BOOKS
New York   London   Toronto   Sydney

An *Original* Publication of POCKET BOOKS

A Pocket Star Book published by
POCKET BOOKS, a division of Simon & Schuster, Inc.
1230 Avenue of the Americas, New York, NY 10020

ISBN: 0-7434-9756-2

First Pocket Books printing February 2005

10 9 8 7 6 5 4 3 2 1

POCKET STAR BOOKS and colophon are registered trademarks of Simon & Schuster, Inc.

Interior design by Davina Mock

Manufactured in the United States of America

For information regarding special discounts for bulk purchases, please contact Simon & Schuster Special Sales at 1-800-456-6798 or business@simonandschuster.com.

One

Outside, an overcast sky blanketed the Jensen house in darkness. No stars shone; no bright moon lit the semirural landscape. Only the house's own lights made a half-hearted attempt to illuminate the dark world—light spilling from windows where the curtains were partly drawn, light from the glass-enclosed bulb beside the front door. At night, Tim Jensen liked to be inside the house, where lamps could be switched on with the flick of a finger or the twist of a knob. Where the shadows could easily be chased away.

Tim was eight years old, and he hated the dark. The only enemy that even came close was homework. He sat on the floor in the family's bright kitchen, struggling through a reading assignment that was open in his lap, as his father worked under the sink.

Tim was glad it was the old man and not him—being jammed halfway inside a cupboard like that would have made him nervous. Scared him to death, really. Tim understood he was just a little kid (but getting bigger all the time, penciled scores on the doorjamb to his room proved that) and that little kids sometimes were afraid of strange things. But cupboards and closets—where darkness seemed to dwell, as if it grew inside them and crept out to overtake the rest of the house when the lights went off—were definitely not his thing.

"Nocturnal predators of the forest . . . ?" he sounded out, wondering even as he spoke the words if he was pronouncing them close to correctly. That was the thing with this reading deal. He could figure out how he thought the words should sound, but half the time what he came up with wasn't anywhere near right, and then he was embarrassed to discover just how far off he was.

A hand flopped out from under the sink. Big knuckles, long fingers streaked with black, nails bitten to the quick. Black under the nails, too. Working man's hands, that's what his dad called them. "Channel locks," the old man said. He might as well have been sounding out something for himself, as far as Tim was concerned. *Channel locks? What are they? Something to do with the TV?* No, his dad wanted a tool of some kind—he'd been doing this for twenty minutes, acting like one of those doctors on television performing an operation. Tim scanned the toolbox looking for something that might be channel locks. Process of elimination. He knew hammers, screwdrivers, wrenches, pliers. Lot of other, less familiar items were crowded in with those, however.

And while he searched, another question weighed on his mind. "Dad, what does 'nocturnal' mean?"

There, that had to be it. At least, it looked like it might lock down on something. He passed it to his dad, hoping it was right. He didn't want to tick off the old man. Just a voice and a hand and some legs, right now, stained jeans and Nikes, but that was all he needed to terrorize Tim when he had a mad on.

He might not even need the legs. Those arms, those hands, were pretty darn scary by themselves.

Instead of "thanks," or answering the question, Dad grumped, "Ask your mom."

As if on cue, Mom shoved open the door from the back hall with a laundry basket full of folded clothes. " 'Nocturnal' means staying up all night," she explained patiently. "Something you're not going to do." She put the basket down on the table. If there was one thing Mom was good at, it was folding laundry. Crisp. She could have taught soldiers how to get good sharp creases. But there were a lot more things she did well, Tim knew. He was crazy about his mom; like an angel, she was, a beacon of light in a dark, dark world. Tim watched her go to the cupboard, take out a glass, and fill it from a pitcher of water they kept on the counter.

Dad chose that moment to extricate himself from under the sink. No, Tim decided, he had been wrong. The whole package was infinitely scarier than the voice and hands by themselves. Just the way he glanced at Tim, eyes dark and flashing with perceived rage, hair greasy, jaw stubbled, face streaked with sweat and grease, made the boy nervous. Dad had no reason to be angry—Tim was just doing his homework, and trying to hand over the correct tools when called upon to do so. But lack of a reason had never stopped the old man before. Tim was glad Mom was there. She could be a calming influence, sometimes. "I need the basin wrench from my toolbox," Dad said.

Tim started to reach for it, nocturnal animals forgotten for the moment, but Mom stepped between him and the box. She wore a dress, as she almost always did. Or maybe it was a skirt. Tim knew he was sometimes described as "precocious," and he thought it meant something like smart, but for the life of him he could never remember the difference between a dress and a skirt. Either way, her legs were suddenly between him and the toolbox, like fleshy prison bars. "Your dad can get his own basin wrench."

Which Tim (precocious, after all) understood translated as, "go get ready for bed." Before he could budge, though, the phone rang. The old man had been talking for as long as Tim could remember about putting an extension in the kitchen, but he hadn't done so yet.

Tugging himself to his feet with his left hand gripping the edge of the sink, Dad looked at Mom—a variation on the same glare he'd turned on Tim just seconds ago, like he was looking for a reason to get mad at someone and just hadn't found it yet. "You expecting a call?"

It didn't matter if she was, obviously. The old man liked to be the one to answer the phone, especially at night. Mom shrugged, and he blew through the kitchen door to grab it, hauling the toolbox with him. The phone wouldn't wait, but apparently neither would that basin wrench. Mom shrugged again, a small one, for Tim's benefit, and handed him the glass of water, kissing the top of his head as she did so. She smelled like a flower garden, sweet and earthy at the same time. He loved her aroma. "Good night, Tim," she said.

"Night, Mom."

Which was the dismissal he had known was coming. He would read about nocturnal animals for a few minutes in bed, maybe, before he went to sleep. He tucked the book under his arm, took the water, and followed his dad's path, out into the hall, toward the stairs and his room.

To reach the stairs he had to pass by his dad, who stood with the phone snugged between ear and shoulder, rummaging through the toolbox with his hands. "I'll ask him," he said into the phone. "Hold up a sec, buddy."

That was to Tim, who froze with one hand on the banister. He turned back to his dad expectantly. He felt like his veins had turned to ice water, and suddenly he really needed to go to the bathroom.

"Call you later, Jack." Dad hung up the phone, which was as far from its usual spot in the living room as its long cord would allow. Jack was a neighbor down the street, Tim knew. Which could only mean bad news.

Tim started to feel a flush coming over him, tried to will it back. *Don't act like you did anything wrong,* he told himself. *Act like it's just any other night . . .*

But his dad came up with the basin wrench, and then his full attention riveted on Tim. "You didn't lose your Roberto Clemente baseball, did you?"

Tim tried to control his breathing, his posture, anything the old man might be able to use as a lie detector. But he didn't answer—words wouldn't come to him at this moment. Instead he wiggled his shoulders in what he hoped was a casual shrug.

"Mr. Krutchmer found one in his house." Dad paused to let that sink in. When Tim didn't reply, he continued. "On the wrong side of the living room window."

Tim forced out a response. Squeaky and flat. "No. I didn't lose it." *I knew right where it was the whole time,* he didn't add. No sense intentionally antagonizing Dad. Unintentionally was bad enough.

"You weren't playing catch with Katie in his front yard?"

Of course I was, Tim thought. *His yard is flat, with plenty of grass. Perfect for it. Katie throws like a girl but she's a good catch.* He'd been the one who missed—it had bounced off the tips of his fingers and sailed into the window. They had both watched, paralyzed with fear, and then before the glass finished tinkling to the floor inside they took off running. "No."

"You sure?" Like that would work. Dad's little out—like if Tim changed his mind and confessed, he wouldn't get in trouble. Like that bogus story about George Washington and the cherry tree. Even at eight, Tim was sure that was a crock. If young George had actually chopped down that tree, it was a safe bet his old man had walloped him. The honest confession only worked on TV sitcoms, and those dads weren't his. When it came to dealing with Tim's father, absolute denial was the only hope. "You know what happens to bad little children who lie to their parents?"

"Yeah." No question about that. Dad's theories on the subject were well known, and Tim didn't especially want to be reminded.

"All right. Go to bed." The old man nodded toward the stairs. Tim didn't have to be told twice. He had thought for a horrible moment that this evening, perfectly pleasant, in the warm embrace of his family, would turn into one of those other kinds of evenings. The kind where . . .

Never mind. It hadn't. The stairs were high and dark and Tim didn't like going up them—too many shadows, and how could you trust shadows? But his room was up there, so he did. At the top, first door on the right, Tim stopped off in the bathroom to brush his teeth and wash his face. Those tasks done, he carried the water glass and the animal book into his room. He had left the lights on, but someone had come by and turned them off, he guessed.

He flipped the switch by the door, turning on the overhead light. Then he crossed to the lamp on his bedside table, clicked it on as well, and put down the glass of water. With light flooding the room, chasing shadows, he changed into his Ninja Turtles pajamas. When the old man was on a rampage, this room could be a haven, a place of safety and comfort. All his best stuff was kept in here: his baseball bat and glove (but not his ball, anymore), a box of assorted trading cards, a couple of model rocket ships his dad had helped him build. He had his books, his comics, his toys. Action figures posed on one of his bookshelves, and Tim's own drawings were taped to the walls. Turning off the overhead light, he clambered into bed. Took a breath. Swallowed hard.

He switched off the bedside lamp.

Darkness filled the room; shadows took over.

Through parted curtains and a window he had left open about three inches, moonlight painted a pale block on one wall. A strange shape jutted into the middle of it, like some kind of threatening weapon. *It's just a branch from the tree outside*, Tim told himself. *It's just a branch*.

But he didn't like the looks of it, not one bit.

Another odd shape loomed on his bedside table, close enough to strike without warning. He started, then got a better look, realizing it was a He-Man action figure that he had left standing there. Trying to calm the pounding of his heart, he yanked open the drawer of his bedside table and tipped the toy inside.

At the foot of the bed, a nebula ball gave off its own minimal light, the current inside sparking and warping like a snake plugged into an electrical outlet. Suspended above, its underside washed in the nebula ball's faint glow, a black mechanical bird caught a slight breeze that wafted in through the window, a breeze scented with night-blooming flowers that climbed a trellis outside. In the breeze, the bird flapped its wings once, then stopped.

The nighttime world of the eight-year-old. In the dark, the veil between worlds was thin; anything could come to life. Anything could happen.

Tim felt his hands begin to tremble under the covers.

And across the room, his closet door creaked open.

He caught his breath, held it, trying to see through the gloom without opening his eyes more than the tiniest slits. If he opened his eyes wide, it would see him— *whatever* it was. In the nightstand he kept a flashlight for emergencies. Its beam, he was sure, could keep anything at bay. Quickly, he spun under the covers, tugging open the same drawer into which he'd tossed He-Man, got a grip on the light. Before he could click it on, though, the closet door closed again. A dark form stared at him from near the closet, and Tim's lower lip started to quiver.

There was someone in here with him.

He turned the flashlight on and aimed it at the form, as if it were a ray gun.

It was nothing. His own bathrobe and some grass-stained jeans tossed over the back of his desk chair. *You're being stupid, Jensen*, he told himself.

He held the flashlight beam on it anyway, only half convinced. Watched for it to change back into a man.

But then the light in his fist flickered, died, and Tim thought his heart would leap out his mouth and scurry under his pillow. Hazarding a glance back toward the chair, he saw that the form—no longer just discarded laundry and furniture—was standing, undeniably the shape of a human.

Tim knew that man's name. His dad had told it to him many times. Told him, too, that it was just a story, that the man wasn't real.

But there he was.

And he was coming for Tim.

Tim tried to scream but couldn't; his voice snagged in his throat like a belch he couldn't vocalize. Only one chance now. He pawed at the bedside light, got it turned on.

As light sped across the room, pushing shadow before it, Tim's robe and jeans fell to the floor, a pile of laundry.

But they were on the chair before, he told himself. *I know they were.*

And now they're . . . they're not. Why would they have fallen, unless . . .

He didn't even want to follow that thought.

Tim braved the floor, despite the chance that something might snag his ankles from under the bed, and dove toward the wayward clothing. He scooped the jeans and robe up and jammed them into a dresser drawer. Grabbed the chair on which the clothes had so recently rested and muscled it over to the dresser, shoving its back up under the dresser drawer knob.

Tim started to turn back to the bed, but something moved there, behind him. He just caught a glimpse, from the corner of his eye as he turned, just heard the slightest rustle. But it was enough to know.

Something was over there, between him and the relative safety of his bed.

And before he could turn the rest of the way around to see it, the bedside lamp clicked off.

Panic overtook him then. Flashlight out, bedside lamp gone, something in the room with him. Something malevolent—nice things didn't hang out in the dark, in the rooms of little kids—and growing bigger.

Tim backed away from the bed and whatever was on it, or in it, or maybe under it. But that meant backing toward the closet.

And behind him, he knew with absolute certainty, the closet door was now open. He could feel it back there. He spun around.

Wide open.

The shadow man stood just inside the closet, right in the front, where, thanks to the moon and the open curtains, the darkness wasn't quite total.

Tim dove. If the man was in the closet, then he wasn't at the bed any longer. Tim hit the bed, shaking, certain that any second would be his last. Trying to bury himself under his sheets, he whipped out an arm that sent his water glass sailing off the nightstand. It hit the hardwood floor, shattering wetly. Nothing he could do about that. It wasn't safe out there. He burrowed under the covers. The only protection he had was the sheet over his head, and there was just enough light out in the dark room for Tim to see that the safety its thin fabric provided wasn't sufficient. The shadow form closed on him, an arm reaching out, a hand grasping the fabric.

Yanking it away.

The scream, stuck in Tim's craw for so long, finally erupted.

"What're you doing?"

Dad. Not a shadow being, not some malevolent entity after all. Or, if malevolent, then only in the human way, not in the supernatural way he had feared. Tim instantly felt ashamed for being so scared, for screaming like that.

But he *had* been here, was no doubt still hiding in the shadows, just waiting for Dad to leave. "He's here!"

"Who's here?"

"He came out of the closet." Tim knew he was blubbering, almost hysterical, but he couldn't contain his terror. He didn't know if his father had come in because he had heard Tim scream, or for some other reason . . . some briefly delayed punishment for the baseball incident, perhaps. Didn't really matter, anyway. The old man hated signs of weakness in his son, and a nighttime scream could earn its own punishment.

Dad tried to sound calm, reasonable. "Nobody's here, Tim," he said. "What're you talking about?"

Tim didn't understand why his dad was playing dumb. He *knew* who it was—the only person the shadow man could possibly be. Tim didn't want to say the name out loud, though; he was certain that if he did that, it would be the last sound he ever uttered. The shadow man wouldn't sit still and let Tim name him.

Finally he beckoned his dad closer and whispered the word in his ear.

Dad's grin was not as soothing as he probably intended for it to be. Instead, it looked phony, like the smile of one of those salesmen on TV, pushing some goofy kitchen tool no one would ever really use. That grin was almost as scary as the darkness itself. "Oh," Dad said. "That was just a story. He's not real."

Tim nodded, like he was believing the line his dad was handing out. Dads tried to calm their kids down when they got scared, everyone knew that. And the way to calm kids down was to tell them their fears weren't real. How many times had Tim heard that one?

But *that* was the story. The truth was already out.

Dad could tell Tim wasn't buying it. "Let's have a look," he said. He went to the bedroom door, standing open since he had come in, and pulled it away from the wall. "Not behind the door."

He knelt on the floor—Tim moved to the edge of his bed, to look down without getting off it—and lifted the dust ruffle, peering underneath. "Not under the bed."

But all this was just stalling, killing time. Tim knew where the shadow man was. He raised a quaking arm and pointed toward the closet. He didn't trust his own voice to speak.

"Right," Dad said. He moved to the closet with all the confidence in the world. *It must be great to be a grown-up*, Tim thought. *Fearless. Believing so absolutely in the nonexistence of the world's terrors. I can't wait till I'm there.*

His dad stepped into the closet and pushed around

Tim's clothes. "No, not here either," he said. He *sounded* sure.

But I saw him in there, Tim wanted to say. *I know he was there.*

His dad wouldn't believe him, though. Having looked with his own eyes, he would be more convinced by that than by Tim's equally positive knowledge that since he *was* in there, he *had* to be in there still.

Dad turned away from the closet, his mind already made up, so he wasn't looking when the shape emerged from the pitch-black shadows behind him. A tall shape, darkness wrapped in night.

But Tim saw it, and he felt terror clamp his heart. "Dad!" he screamed.

Darkness lanced out toward Tim's father, an arm of pure black, a shadow tentacle. It looped around Dad and yanked him off his feet, backward.

Into the closet.

"DAD!" Tim shrieked. He couldn't yell any louder— *Where's Mom?* he wondered briefly. *Why hasn't she come running?*

But she was probably down in the laundry room. Or else she was just used to Tim being afraid of things in the dark.

Almost as if in response to his scream, Dad flew out of the closet, as if some inhuman force had fired him from a cannon. He slammed into the floor, hard. Tim felt his bed jump from the impact. Dad groaned and clawed at the wooden floor. But whatever was in there still had him by his feet, his ankles. As his father's hands scratched uselessly at the wooden floor, that something drew him back inside, inch by inch.

At the last moment, Dad's outflung hands grasped the doorjamb, halting his disappearance into the closet's depths. Tim could see his father's face, eyes popping with the effort, skin flushed, veins bulging. His dad was scared, really truly scared in a way that Tim hadn't realized grown-ups could ever be. But still, he fought.

Tim realized maybe that was the difference between kids and grown-ups, or between the fearful and the courageous. He was safe on the bed, and yet he was petrified, rooted to the spot. His dad was being hauled into a dark closet by a monster, and he struggled to save himself.

But Dad's efforts were for nothing. The closet door, seemingly of its own accord, began slamming into him, over and over and over. With each slam, Tim heard sickening noises—the tearing of flesh, the splintering of bone. Still, his dad held fast. As if wearying of this effort, whatever held Dad suddenly hurled him upward, driving him into the top of the door frame, and then dropped him back to the floor. Tim's dad cried out in agony and lost his grip.

And then, as quickly as a feather being sucked into a vacuum hose, he was yanked into the closet. A quick scream, a flurry of motion. He was there, he was gone. That fast.

The closet door stood open like a laughing mouth, mocking Tim, for a second longer. A distant noise trickled out. It sounded miles away, seeping into Tim's room from across some incredible distance—a kind of rushing sound, like a roaring waterfall.

And then the door slammed shut and the room was absolutely silent. As still as if none of it had ever happened. Moonlight on the wall, mechanical bird motionless in the air, water pooling on the floor where Tim had knocked over his glass.

Tim, alone on his bed, whimpering like a wounded puppy.

Fatherless.

Two

The offices of *End Magazine* were decorated in a curious mix of styles. High-tech, modern furnishings and state-of-the-art hardware—especially for the graphics people—were thrown together with discount office furniture and cut-rate cubicles, all surrounded by walls and floors that would have benefited from a coat of paint or a carpet shampoo, or even just some cleanser and a rag. But the magazine life was a high-pressure one, deadline driven and bare bones. Paying a crew to do more than the most basic maintenance—emptying wastebaskets, sweeping the floors—wasn't in the budget, and no one on staff had time to worry about such things.

Even today, the day before the Thanksgiving holiday, Jessica Brittan could barely pry herself free from her workload to make it to Pam Cartwright's good-bye party. Magazine deadlines didn't care about holidays or staff changes, and Jessica had to design three articles before the end of the month. Two of the three needed photos. Jessica's old Mac had been a faithful friend, but lately it was giving her fits, especially when she called upon it to work with really large files. It crawled. Sometimes it froze up completely, and if she hadn't been saving her work regularly she lost time and trouble. She had already put in a request for a new computer, but ad sales had been a little flat lately and she had been told that she would have to wait for another few months.

By the time she got out of her office, the party was going strong. Jessica bumped into a little knot of coworkers standing on the fringes of it all, drinks in hand—some emptier than others. On Jason Bates, at least, a flushness of face and a strange dipping of one shoulder toward the wall—as if he was leaning on it when, in fact, it was at least eight inches away—indicated that several drinks had already come and gone.

Across the room, a makeshift bar had been put together on an empty desk that had once belonged to another casualty of the ad rate situation. Not everyone who left the magazine was replaced, and as a result there were a few empty spots around the bullpen. Pam had an office, not a cubicle, and her resignation had prompted a massive controversy among the cubicle dwellers over who got to inherit her space.

Jessica's boyfriend. Tim Jensen—handsome, midtwenties, clean-shaven, longish brown hair that she loved to curl and tease with her fingertips hanging over his ears—stood in front of the bar with a couple of friends, glaring at a vodka bottle. His empty glass stood on the desk before him. "This is going to turn ugly," he warned. He upended the bottle over the glass and poured a few drops (less than a shot, for sure) into it. "That's the last of the vodka."

"What are you doing for Thanksgiving?" Tanya asked, distracting Jessica from Tim's vodka woes for the moment.

"You know," Jessica said. "Family, turkey, gaining ten pounds. Tim's coming over."

Tanya grabbed Jessica's arm and leaned close. Her booze breath reminded Jessica of a medicine bottle. "Holiday with the 'rents? That's a big step."

"He feels like he's ready for it," Jessica replied. She'd maybe had to push a little, but not too much; she didn't think she was forcing him into anything, at least. And she hated to think about him spending the holiday alone.

Tanya started to say something else, but Jessica tuned her out. Pam Cartwright, guest of honor at this shindig, was working her way though the crowd toward Tim and the other guys holding court at the bar. Pam was pretty, if a little too much in the make-sure-everyone-notices kind of way, and even though she'd had a few, she wasn't too far gone to forget to use her slinky, attention-grabbing walk as she pushed to the front. As if the walk wouldn't do the trick by itself, her lavender blouse was tight and her skirt showed plenty of long leg. "Tim, let me have one of those green things?" she asked.

"Sour apple martini?" Tim said. There were a few already mixed on the desk, and he handed one over to her. Pam smiled broadly and took a sip of the concoction.

"Tastes like candy," she said happily.

Jason Bates had left Jessica's little clutch as soon as the conversation had turned toward Thanksgiving plans, and he wove his way unsteadily toward the bar. As Pam was turning away, he lurched past her and bumped into her arm. Some of her sour apple martini sloshed out of her glass and onto the floor. "Careful," Jason said. Too little, too late.

"Oops!" The collision launched Pam into a loud giggling fit.

"That's it," Jason said, trying to snatch her glass out of her hand. "No more for Pam!"

She dodged his grab, almost spilling more but managing to keep it contained. *She's not quite as drunk as she acts*, Jessica thought. Most of the time, she liked Pam, but the girl had a definite center-of-attention thing going. "Hey, it's my party!" she declared, defending her drink from Jason's attempts.

Jason shrugged and turned to Tim. "Tim, you going to be around this weekend?"

Finally, Tim's brown eyes caught Jessica's gaze. He smiled and held out a hand to her, and she started toward him. She had always been drawn to his eyes, and she couldn't resist them now even if she had wanted to. "I thought I'd see if I could wrangle a dinner invitation from one of those art department girls," he said. "Like this one right here."

Reaching him, Jessica breathed in his scent—even

mixed with the alcohol, she loved his musky aroma—and kissed him on the mouth. "Did Tim tell you about meeting my parents tomorrow?" she asked Jason.

"Whoa, meeting the folks," Jason said. "This is serious."

Pam Cartwright rested a hand lightly on Jessica's shoulder. "If he can survive the weekend with Jessica's father," she added. Jessica stiffened at the sound of Pam's voice. She figured Pam just hadn't wanted to lose the spotlight, so she was trying to become the focus of a conversation that wasn't about her in the least. But Jessica didn't want her father to become topic A among a bunch of coworkers letting off steam.

"Dad's not that bad," she countered.

"Except for the time he tried to drown you," Pam shot back.

Leave it to Pam. Her ploy had worked. Now, once again, all eyes were on her. But Jessica's family was, really, none of Pam's business.

Tim shook his head sympathetically. "You never should have told her that story."

Obviously. But she had to explain, now that Pam had tossed it out there. These were journalists—given a hint of a juicy story, they would pursue it, refusing to let go. "I was seven," she explained. "He was trying to teach me to swim."

"By throwing her into the middle of a lake," Pam elaborated. "She sank straight to the bottom."

"Your dad sounds like fun," Jason said, dripping sarcasm. He gave Tim a brotherly poke in the arm. "Been nice knowing you, Tim." He wandered away, but even with her audience reduced by one, Pam refused to let up. "Then there's Jessica's sister," she went on.

"I think that's enough about my family." Jessica was only half a drink away from substituting something like, *Drop it, bitch.*

"Come on, Jess," Pam pushed. "Just one Chelsea story."

Apparently Jessica should never have told Pam any of her family tales, because the woman seemed to have a steel-trap memory for them. There were, in fact, plenty of Chelsea stories Jessica could have told, most of which were time-tested laugh getters. But they were often embarrassing to Jessica at the same time. The one about Chelsea getting caught with her bridesmaid's dress hiked up around her waist, bent over the table that was meant for the gifts, giving an early wedding present to her best friend's groom, wasn't a bad one—the only reflection on Jessica was that the groom was an ex-boyfriend of hers, who had dumped her for the woman he was about to marry. And the one where Chelsea started dating the state trooper who had pulled Jessica over for speeding was okay too. Most of them were even more obnoxious, like the time in high school when Chelsea had changed the lock on her gym locker, forcing Jessica to attend a geometry test in smelly gym clothes while the janitor cut the lock off.

Rather than tell any of them, however, Jessica was considering the social implications of dumping her drink down Pam's blouse instead of finishing it. But that would only give Pam the wet T-shirt look, and glue even more eyes to her. Before Jessica could make her mind up, Tim came to the rescue, tapping on a beer bottle with a handy letter opener to call for attention. "This might be a good time for a toast," he announced. "Everyone."

The chatter in the room came to a lull, and all eyes turned toward Tim. *Which is no doubt fine with Pam*, Jessica thought, *because she's still the main event.* She had probably timed her last day to be this one so that she could take over the party, make it be about her instead of Thanksgiving. Jessica could tell by Tim's pause that he'd called the toast just to cover her, and hadn't actually planned anything to say. His eyes had a little bit of a deer-in-the-headlights look to them. But after a couple of seconds' reflection, he smiled. "When we get back from Thanksgiving on Monday, this place will be very different," he began. "For starters, it'll be quieter." This drew a laugh from the assembly, and Tim continued. "But it certainly won't be as much fun. All of us at *End*, and particularly in editing, are going to miss Pam and her fat red pen—"

"And her dirty e-mails!" Jason shouted out.

A bigger laugh. Tim smiled and kept talking, glossing over it. "And her willingness to help others, even when she's on deadline." He raised his glass high, in Pam's direction. "The *Daily News* is lucky to get you."

A roar of approval came from the group, with even Jessica joining in. People clinked their glasses together, and then conversation resumed, maybe louder than before. Pam dabbed at her eye with a knuckle, misty all of a sudden. "Tim, you're the nicest person here," she said.

She moved in close, enveloped Tim in her arms, pulling him against her body. She held on for just a little too long, and Jessica stepped in, pretending to be a fight referee.

"Okay," she said, with a mock snarl, "break it up." She playfully separated them, and the two came apart. Pam turned to Jessica and held onto her arms, looking into her eyes with sudden intensity.

"Be good to him, Jess," she said. "He deserves it." Then she let go of Jessica with one hand, and used it to grab Tim again. "I'm going to miss you." She raised her voice. "All of you."

Pam moved away from them, into the crowd where everyone could assure her, one-on-one, how empty their lives would be without her. Jessica didn't want to say "good riddance," but if Pam had pushed any more of her buttons, she might have anyway. She knew Tim wouldn't understand her feelings, and didn't want to let on how much Pam had gotten to her. "Yeah, I'll miss her too," she lied.

Guessing that it was getting late, she glanced at her watch. She had to get out of here, should have been on the road an hour ago. "I told my parents I'd be there by eleven."

"I'll get your coat," Tim volunteered. He headed away from the party, toward her office. Jessica said her good-byes, moving through Pam's wake, wishing everyone a happy Thanksgiving. Glasses were lifted to her. Turkey jokes abounded, along with references to football games and parades. A few people asked about Chelsea, but Jessica promised she'd tell the stories after

Thanksgiving, hoping that everyone would forget by then.

Finally, she freed herself from the thinning throng and went toward her office. Tim still hadn't reappeared with her coat, and she had begun to wonder what was keeping him. When she reached her office, she saw him through the big glass partition, standing trancelike, in front of the open door to her freestanding closet. It was almost as if he'd been hypnotized by something inside. Jessica glanced up and down the corridor, hoping none of their coworkers were witness to Tim's strange behavior. She went inside and touched his shoulder. "Hey."

Tim jumped as if someone had shouted at him. "Jess!" he said, too loud and too fast. "Sorry."

Reaching past him, she took her own coat from the open closet and slipped it on. "You're not getting weird on me again?" She worried about Tim from time to time, though he always seemed to normalize before things got too creepy. If he hadn't, they never would have lasted even this long. She was pretty crazy about him, but she was no social worker. Guys as nice as Tim were hard to find, especially when they were also handsome. But head cases were a dime a dozen.

"I just spaced out for a minute," he explained.

Maybe so. He'd had a few drinks, after all. Maybe more than a few—as bartender, he had been at the party since its beginning. That could have put him off balance. "Okay." She smiled, wrapping an arm around his. "Shall we make an exit?"

Outside, he walked her toward the parking garage with his own coat on and his backpack slung over his shoulder. He looked normal enough, but there was still something going on with him, she thought. More than just the drinks. Something on his mind. He was silent, lost in his own thoughts, barely acknowledging her presence beside him. "Hey, you okay?" she asked.

"Yeah, I'm fine." He was trying to sound convincing, but didn't quite pull it off.

"You're being kinda quiet."

Tim stopped, pulled her toward him, fully engaged at last. "I think I just drank a little too much. C'mere, I'll show you I'm okay." He wrapped his arms around her, drawing her close. His lips found hers, his tongue slipping past her teeth. He tasted of booze, but at least he was *with* her again, not off in outer space by himself. After a minute, he broke the clench and smiled hopefully. She nodded, letting him know that she accepted the demonstration.

"I can't believe I have to drive all the way out there tonight," she complained as they hurried toward the garage. The night was cold; stars glinted in the dark sky like chips of ice. She had foregone alcohol herself, knowing the long drive awaited, and she couldn't wait to get inside the car and get the heater going.

Inside the garage, her silver BMW was one of the only cars in sight. "Where's your car?" she asked Tim.

"It wouldn't start."

A flash of suspicion ignited in her. She hoped this wasn't some kind of scam to get out of coming to her parents' house. "Is it gonna make it tomorrow?"

"I got a guy looking at it."

She pressed the button on her remote. The BMW

unlocked, its inside light coming on. She loved its sleek lines and precise German engineering. "Tim, if you think you're gonna use the 'car broke down' excuse to get out of this . . ." She left her threat unspoken.

"I'll be there," he assured her. His face was serious in the half-light of the garage, his gaze locked on hers. "I promise."

"Okay," she relented. Puppy dog eyes, that's what he had. That's why she always cut him slack when he asked for it. He knew it, too, and used them as weapons. "You want a ride home?"

"Nah, I'm good," Tim replied. "I'll cut through the park. It's a ten minute walk."

She knew he was right, and knew the cold wouldn't be a problem for him. *Probably be good for him,* she thought. *Sober him up a little.* "All right," she said, kissing him again. "Be careful."

Jessica got into the car, hoping he really was okay. She cared for Tim, a lot. Probably more than she ever had about any other guy. Bringing him home for the holiday proved that; she'd never taken any previous relationship that far. They hadn't talked about forever, yet, except in the most vague terms. Someday we'll go to French Polynesia together. Someday we'll have a place in the country. Stuff like that. French Polynesia was her idea—Tim had a thing about wanting to visit Alaska, north of the Arctic Circle, during summer. The sun doesn't go down for more than a month, he had said, as if that was some big selling point.

She cared for him—loved him, she figured, when she allowed herself to even think about that word—but she also worried about him, and at the back of her mind a niggling fear never quite went away. She was afraid that someday the worry would overwhelm the caring.

Not yet, though. He gave a friendly wave, blew a kiss, and strode away confidently. *Maybe I'm just being overprotective. He's fine. A couple drinks too many, but fine.*

She started the car, letting it idle for a minute, and watched him disappear into the dark.

Three

Tim felt the cold air waking him up as he walked the dark, quiet streets. The city seemed to have turned in early, maybe everyone saving up energy for the big day tomorrow. There were still a few people out, but not nearly as many as there would have been on a normal weekday evening. He actually would have liked a ride from Jessica, but he wanted to clear his head, to get over his senior moment in front of her closet. *Don't know what happened there,* he thought. *Just . . . well, it's a closet. Dark inside.*

Bad news.

He didn't like the dark, not a bit. He never had. He didn't like closets, either. The combination of the two was just more than he could deal with sometimes. He hated that Jess had seen it. He knew she was already a little concerned about his mental state. He strove for normalcy, especially around her. She was the best thing that had come his way in years, and he really, really didn't want to blow it. She was sweet, funny, drop-dead gorgeous. A very talented artist and designer. As smart as anyone he had ever known. He couldn't stand the idea that he might someday drive her away with his stupid little phobia.

Glancing at the sidewalk ahead, he noticed a city utility door set into a brick wall, its surface marred by the ragged shreds of old posters and handbills. Concerts that had already come and gone, a play running in one of the downtown theatres, "Have You Seen This Boy?" The kind of wall-plastering detritus common to every city.

But the door hung open, which it shouldn't have. The city wouldn't have anyone working in there, not on the night before a holiday, unless it was some kind of emergency. Tim looked around. The streets were bright with holiday lights: flashing, blinking, every color imaginable sparkling from shop windows, apartments, lampposts. Neons, fluorescents, incandescents. Even cars on the road or stopped at traffic lights got into the act—in addition to their headlights and taillights, some had extra holiday lights mounted on grills or strung on roof racks.

One thing Tim Jensen noticed was lights, and they were on here. No power failure or other emergency that he could see.

But another thing he was attuned to was dark places, and that door was open, no doubt about it, and behind it, inside the utility closet, he saw nothing but shadow.

Tim swallowed, suddenly nervous. There was something very not right about this scene. He cast his gaze this way and that, hoping someone else had noticed the door, or that maybe a workman would show up to close it. But the street was nearly empty, and none of the handful of people Tim could see paid it any attention at all. Tim was the only one who seemed to have spotted the door, the only one who cared.

He drew closer. Turning back and going around this block would cost him another ten minutes, at least, double the time home. Tim considered it anyway, but then decided against it. Too much trouble, too cold out.

Too dark out.

It's just an open door, he told himself. *Just walk past it. Just a door.*

An open door that captivated his attention. As he approached, he couldn't look away.

And in one of those sudden, unpredictable moments when all the city's noises—traffic, TVs, conversations, the rumble and roar of millions of people pushed together—come to a brief hush all at once, he heard it.

A low, groaning sound came from inside the utility closet.

It was like nothing he'd ever heard—maybe the noise an injured rhino would make. Tim shuddered and stepped up his pace. *Is there something inside?* he wondered. All he could see was blackness, empty and infinite. As he passed by it, he heard the groan again, and it was like the fingers of death's hand tripped lightly down his spine. It took everything Tim had not to break into a sprint. Finally, a dozen or so feet beyond the gaping black maw, he risked a glance behind him.

Someone stood at the open doorway. Dark, indistinct, as if he was made of shadow, warped and twisted in unskilled hands into a shape only vaguely reminiscent of humanity. *He can't be real,* Tim thought, *no one could look like that for real.* Tim turned around again, eyes front. *Watch where you're going, Timmy. And next time, don't drink so damn much. Hallucinations are a bad sign.*

No one called him Timmy. Even when he'd been a kid, it had almost always been Tim. Very occasionally, his mom had used Timmy, but usually he was just Tim unless she was pissed at him, and then it had been Timothy. Never his dad or his friends. He guessed he just had never seemed like a Timmy. But the voice inside his head, the one that berated him when he was stupid, that warned him when he was about to burn his fingers or step into traffic—that voice *always* called him Timmy.

The strange thing was, that voice sounded a little like his dad. Or like a cross between himself and his dad. As an adult, Tim had never heard his father's voice, and he had often wondered how alike they might have sounded, if the old man had still been around.

A couple of blocks farther, the mouth of an alley loomed. Out here on the street, the lampposts and windows and holiday lights kept the shadows mostly at bay. But the alley, long and lit only by incidental illumination from the street, was dark. Tim hurried past its mouth, hazarding a single glance down its length. Black, oily puddles on the ground, ladders and strange latticework above, sheer, unbroken walls all around. Steam billowed from vents he couldn't see. Not for a million bucks would he walk down it at night.

He was almost past the alley when he heard that moaning sound again. He missed a step, almost tripped, but caught himself. There was a different undertone to it this time—as if the invisible animal, though wounded, still held a grudge against whoever had injured it. This was a fierce growl, not rhino-ish in the least. Predatory.

Curious in spite of his apprehension, Tim stopped, peering into the gloom. The clouds of steam were too thick, the darkness beyond them too absolute. He couldn't see—

Two dogs, black but for bared white teeth and a white blaze on one's chest, tumbled from the steam, snapping and growling, each intent on getting a piece of the other. Tim dodged the duet of dogflesh, picking up his pace again as he moved away.

He had gone beyond apprehension now, toward something very like fear. Things were *wrong* tonight, somehow. The world had slipped its axis, passed through gamma rays. Or he'd stepped through a curtain and was looking back on it from the other side. He couldn't quite put his finger on what was wrong, but everything seemed more menacing than it should have, as if danger waited at every step.

There was no way out of it, though. He needed to get home, and because he had let Jessica go, that meant negotiating the nighttime city. Ahead, he had a choice of two paths: through a small park, which would cut off almost four blocks, or around it. Going through saved time, which meant he'd be home that much sooner. At home, he would be safe, in control. He would have light on his side.

Making up his mind, he climbed the steps and entered the park. Almost instantly, the world smelled different—the downtown stink of exhaust and trash and baked concrete giving way to the rich, fertile smells of earth, the crisp odors of fall foliage. The grass had been cut today and that added another layer, making Tim think of summer evenings when the light hung around until late.

Tim usually enjoyed the park, even at night, as much as he liked any place at night. Sodium vapor lamps cast soft yellow light toward the ground, somehow without splashing light into the sky like ordinary incandescents. He knew that astronomers preferred them, that their glow didn't prevent telescopes from seeing into deep space, like the white wash from other types of bulbs did. He had heard complaints (part of editing a magazine was that one became partially knowledgeable in a lot of diverse areas, and expert in almost none) that they changed colors on the ground too much, making it hard for people to identify others, muggers, and so on. Every kind of light, he figured, had its advocates and its detractors.

For his part, he wasn't overly partial. He just liked light in general.

The thick black shadows behind the trees were

threatening, but the light etched the branches themselves nicely, creating, to Tim's eyes, a kind of modern
art piece. It was ordinarily quiet in here, the sounds of
city traffic filtered by the trees and dampened by grass.

Tonight, though, a strange noise disturbed the park's
normal quiet. This was not like the weird moan he'd
heard earlier, or the racket the fighting dogs made.
After a moment, Tim realized it was the electronic fuzz
of walkie-talkies. Staying on the same path, he topped a
low rise, and saw where it was coming from. Up ahead,
a team of police officers trained flashlights in every direction. The walkie-talkie noise got louder as Tim approached.

Tim thought briefly about turning back, going
around the block after all, but that was silly. He hadn't
done anything wrong. He was a responsible guy, law-
abiding, a hard worker. His taxes paid their salaries. He
kept going. Anyway, he was curious now. What could
they be looking for in here, in the dark?

Ahead, one of the cops stood ramrod-straight, his
hands behind his back, at the edge of the path. He
looked like a soldier waiting for the general's inspection. Beyond him, a guy in a suit sat on a bench talking
to a woman who held her hands over her face, shoulders hunched. The light was dim over there, but Tim
thought she was crying. He stopped next to the cop
who stood by the path. "What's going on?"

The officer's voice was tight, and he wouldn't meet
Tim's gaze. "A missing little boy," he said. "His mom
can't find him." The cop, young and beefy, tried to look
firm and resolute, but Tim thought he detected a

glimmer of moisture in the man's eyes, a slight quivering around the mouth. Whatever had happened, this cop was taking it hard.

Tim found that he was badly shaken as well by this, on top of everything else. Losing a child was one of the worst things he could imagine. Tim wasn't a parent, and didn't know if that was a responsibility he would ever feel ready to take on, but he thought he could well imagine the horror of that loss, such a reversal of his own. He looked for words to say but he couldn't find them. Finally, he settled. "Well, I'll keep an eye out."

"Thanks," the young cop said. "Lots of creeps out here these days."

He turned away and Tim kept heading down the path, the static of walkie-talkies and the piercing beams of flashlights providing accompaniment to his walk. A couple of minutes later, he had left them behind, lost in the woods and the quiet darkness.

As he continued his solitary walk, a lone jogger huffed up the path behind him. Tim was momentarily startled, but that was just because he was so on edge from everything else he had seen and heard tonight. The jogger passed on, and was gone. At the intersection of two paths, Tim passed a young couple, their arms wrapped around each other, oblivious to everything around them.

Tim watched his own breath steam. He pulled his jacket tight against a cold wind that blew skeletal leaves across the walkway, rattling like the bones of the ancient dead.

As he walked, other sounds rose from the night. The

walkie-talkies had faded away, but the sodium vapor lights buzzed dully overhead, and plastic trash bags in their cans rustled in the chill breeze. A distant car horn bleated.

And underneath it all—suddenly, if it had been ongoing he would already have started running—the same deep, groaning sound he had heard before.

Instantly alert, Tim's gaze darted in every direction. There, close to a tree—the same shadowy figure he'd seen before, by the utility closet door? Maybe. This one was dark, just a silhouette, black on black. But the shape looked similar: malformed, twisted, and somehow not quite human. It might have been someone just standing around in the park, at night, the shadows distorting his appearance, but even so, that was a bit odd in itself, wasn't it? Tim stepped up his pace again, all the more anxious to reach the safety of his own apartment.

Before he was even a few steps away, though, he heard another noise, even stranger than the first. It sounded like someone balling up a gigantic piece of aluminum foil, the size of a city block, and it set his teeth on edge just like that would have. A loud, metallic crinkling. He glanced about—something so loud must be huge, he knew, but he couldn't see anything in the dimly lit park that might have made such a sound.

But there was nothing.

Just trees. Shadows. A man standing with his back to Tim, near a trash can. A homeless guy, maybe, scrounging for enough soda cans to buy a late dinner or a drink. He wasn't the strange shadow man. But the crinkling sound continued, louder now, and it was joined by a noise that sounded like a buzz saw ripping through sheet metal, and a clanging as if Tim stood inside a giant bell, and the cacophony was all too loud to be believed. Tim put his hands over his ears, but that just made it worse, like his head would tear apart from the inside out. He started to say something to the homeless guy who just stood there, seemingly oblivious, but if he was really talking he couldn't tell, his own voice was so overwhelmed by the din. Either way, the guy didn't turn around. Tim was starting to wonder if he was one of those lifelike statues, when finally he moved.

At least, his hair moved.

Tim shook his head. None of this was making any sense.

The guy had a mop of greasy black hair, and it slowly parted—though no fingers were touching it. Little by little, it moved.

Revealing a pair of dark, malevolent eyes, looking at Tim. He couldn't have said why but he got the sense that they were challenging him. He had a momentary flash of Travis Bickle in *Taxi Driver*. *Are you looking at me?*

As quickly as it had come, all the noise died. Absolute silence reigned, broken only by Tim's shallow, frightened breaths. None of this was right, none of it could be happening. But denial would have been a lot easier, Tim guessed, if his senses didn't seem to be working just fine now. He could see the park, the trees, the grass. Stars dotting the sky. He could hear distant

traffic, a horn honking, an airplane streaking past overhead. The right sounds, the proper sights.

Except for the guy with the freaky eyes in the back of
his head, staring at him. And then another blur of motion snared Tim's attention. The shadow man, black
and distorted, moving toward him. If a man could even
survive, so twisted and misshapen, he shouldn't be able
to move as fast as this guy was—covering the ground
toward Tim as fast as a cheetah, as a NASCAR racer.

Tim started walking again, fast, almost a run, his
legs scissoring crisply. He closed his eyes as he went,
screwing them tight, and counted on his fingers as he
did. One, two, three, four, five . . .

Risked a glance over his shoulder.

The shadow man wasn't there. Someone else, someone who could have been the homeless guy with the
extra eyes, except that he looked normal now, walked
along pushing a shopping cart full of plastic bags and
aluminum cans. Tim shook his head once again, knowing as he did that it wouldn't help a bit. Either he was
going nuts and imagining all this stuff, or . . .

. . . well, *there isn't really a better option, is there,
Timmy?*

*You're crazy, or the whole world is. You like that any
better? You want to be the last sane one?*

That, Tim knew, was the most unlikely scenario of
the evening. He'd been called a lot of things in his life.
Sane wasn't usually one of them.

Four

Tim never thought he would be so glad to leave the park. Until tonight, he had really enjoyed his experiences in there. Now he wasn't sure he ever would again. He left it behind as fast as he could, hurrying the last couple of blocks to his apartment. When he got there, he jammed his key into the lock, turned it, then repeated the process in the other two dead bolts. Finally, the door swung open and he was home. He reached inside, flipped on the wall switch. Light blazed.

Home was safety. His loft was light and open by day, and at night he had his lamps positioned just right to chase away any shadows that might have tried to encroach on his turf.

The loft was all one big room. Kitchen on one side, cabinets open to the light. Everything was neatly arranged, orderly. Glasses arrayed nicely, plates stacked just so, flatware and utensils in clean plastic baskets. In his sleeping corner, his mattress rested right on the floor, so there could be no shadows—or anything else—beneath it. His closet was open to the room, clothes hanging precisely. Another open-faced cabinet held carefully folded underwear, T-shirts, socks. Shoes in a straight line on the closet floor. A visitor, a writer who sometimes worked for Tim, had once said that it looked like Tim had taken his red pen to his own apartment and excised everything that was out of place, everything extraneous, just as he had done to that writer's last article.

He hadn't been far off. But Tim knew the motivation wasn't quite the same. His place was organized this way for a reason, but that reason wasn't editorial precision or Eastern simplicity.

As Tim walked around the loft, switching on lamps, the light from his array spilled into every corner, every nook. Tim's goal was the banishment of shadows, of dark spots. Of places where something—anything—could hide.

This was his sanctuary, after all. This was where he came to get away from the world and its dangers. This was where light ruled, and the darkness was not invited.

He snatched the phone from its cradle, ignoring the glowing red 1 telling him he had a message, and dialed a number he knew well. While it rang, he helped himself to a beer from the refrigerator and popped it open. The fridge had one door he allowed to be closed, and he tried to pretend he was fine with that, but that one time the bulb in there had burned out, all the food had spoiled before he'd been able to bring himself to change it.

Beep. Leave a message. "Hey, Jane. It's Tim. Jensen. Are you there?" *Apparently not, Einstein.* "No? Listen, I'm . . . uh . . . I don't know if it's 'cause it's the holidays or 'cause I'm going to meet Jessica's parents or what, but I'm . . ." How to describe it? Stark raving bonkers? He decided to take a more subtle approach. "I'm feeling a little more messed up than usual. What's new, right?"

Because that would reassure her, wouldn't it?

"Anyway . . . I was hoping you had some time to see me. Thanks. Bye."

He hung up the phone. What if she *did* have time? What if she called back tonight, or tomorrow morning? How would Jessica take it if he said he had to blow off Thanksgiving with the family because he was afraid he was going batty and had to see his shrink?

But then, how would she like it if he came to dinner and started hallucinating? Who knew what he'd see next? Maybe the turkey would get up off the table and dance a jig. Maybe all the female relatives would line up and dance like the Rockettes, and when they turned around they'd all have eyes in the backs of their heads, winking at him.

Yeah, that'd be terrific.

He'd made the call, though, so there was nothing he could do about it now. And anyway, the chances of getting an appointment immediately were slim to none. Calling this week only increased his odds of getting one within the next several weeks. He pressed PLAY on the answering machine, and recognized the voice immediately. *"Tim, it's Uncle Mike. Listen, I know you're having Thanksgiving with your girlfriend and all, but it'd be real nice if you could make it out to see your mom this weekend. She's not doing so well, and . . . you know. It'd be good for her to see you. And I got some stuff for you to sign too. House stuff. All right, that's all."*

His uncle had disconnected then. Not like he could have done much more damage to Tim's already precarious balance. The last thing he needed was a guilt trip about visiting his mother, on top of everything else.

He hated the place she was living, even though Uncle Mike said it was the best place for her, that she couldn't take care of herself at home any more—not that she ever could. He found it depressing to see her there, weak and haggard, looking as if she had already given up and was just waiting around for the end. Whenever he went there, he was treated to a litany of her ailments, and a long list of people she knew who had recently died.

But it was a long weekend. He could try to get out there, try to see her. It was never fun, always difficult. But he supposed she needed it. He probably did too.

Just like sometimes you need a root canal, Timmy. Like sometimes you have to open the fridge, even though the bulb's burned out.

He would try. That was the best he could promise.

The Brittan house was big. No, *big* was too small a word. For that matter, *house* was too small a word. *Manor,* maybe, which was, to Tim's mind, just slightly less grand, less absurdly ostentatious, than a mansion. Either way, the house was *big,* the kind of place where rich people lived their lives that were so different from everyone else's. Tim had known that Jessica came from money, but the realization had never felt as concrete as it did the moment that he parked his battered blue Mustang in front of her house, slotting it between a Bentley and her BMW.

Just to be sure, he checked the address scrawled on his palm before he'd left home that morning with the one on the house. Right place. *And they probably spring for notepads here,* he thought, wiping his hand on the car's upholstery. He gave himself the once-over in the mirror—tie knotted and straight, hair neat, nothing between his teeth. His jacket was navy, shirt white, tie blue with a gold pattern. Khaki pants. As good as it got; nothing else he could do now, short of cosmetic surgery. He grabbed a bottle of wine he'd spent too much money on (too much for him, although in this place they'd probably think it was a trivial expense) and his overnight bag and climbed out of the car.

Before he even reached the front door, Jessica had come out to meet him. He was a little stunned, as he always was, to realize just how beautiful she was. Her straight blond hair caught the sun like a cascade of molten gold. She wore a red silk dress, just this side of formal, and the way it clung to her figure made him think that it had been made just for her. Probably it had. It also made him think that it was a bit too sexy for a family Thanksgiving dinner, but maybe that was just him. At any rate, he found himself grinning widely as she bounded toward him. He dropped the bag, held onto the bottle, and spread his arms, welcoming her into them. She smelled as good as she looked—clean and fresh, with a floral undertone. And she felt even better than that, pressing her body against his as if trying to mold to him.

"Hey," she said, taking the wine from his hand so he could grab his bag. "I see you got the car started. Were the directions okay?"

He instinctively closed his hand, hoping the ink stains were gone. "Perfect," he replied. He hoisted his overnight bag, raised it toward the magnificent structure behind her. "Shouldn't we wait for the bellhop to come take my bag?"

"Shut up," Jessica said with a laugh. A beautiful laugh, Tim thought, to go along with the rest of the package. There were times he couldn't believe his luck, and this moment was one of them. "It's their house, not mine," she continued. "What's with the tie?"

Suddenly self-conscious, the fingers of Tim's free hand went to the knot. "I don't know. I figured . . . meeting the family and all . . . why not, right?"

He released his tie and Jessica grabbed his hand again, squeezed it hard, and began to lead him toward the house. "I like you like you," she said, their private phrase, hearkening back to junior high crushes. "Come on, we'll put your stuff in the guest room."

Thanksgiving dinner was less like ones Tim remembered from his childhood and more like ones he'd only seen in movies and TV shows. His own early years, it had usually just been Tim and his parents with a scrawny bird. Sometimes his mom put on Christmas music, so the silence wouldn't seem so oppressive. By the time food was on the table, Dad had had hours to watch games and drink beer, and his mood was often foul. After he had . . . had gone . . . it had been even worse.

Jessica's family, though, could have been a cast of actors, each and every one attractive, well groomed, and for the most part well mannered. As the meal wore on, Jessica's Uncle Murphy, who was downing wine a little too fast, and her sister Chelsea's three-year-old son Jarod both got a bit tendentious. The meal was exquisite: turkey, of course, with molasses glaze and all the trimmings, cranberry sauce, several kinds of stuffing, mashed potatoes, a variety of fresh vegetables, and buttermilk-sage biscuits—not the kind that came in a tube. The eleven of them gathered around a vast dining table, set with fine bone china, Waterford crystal, and real sterling silver.

Jessica's mom, Arlene, who was definitely a major contributor to her daughter's beauty, Tim discovered, finished her wine (which had apparently, contrary to Tim's expectations, been a popular choice) and Jessica refilled her glass.

"Thank you, dear. Maybe just one more glass. It's very good."

"Tim picked it out," Jessica said.

Arlene gave Tim a smile that looked oddly familiar to Tim, before he realized that it was very similar to Jessica's own flirtatious grin. She held his gaze long enough that he almost felt dirty for thinking how pretty she was. "It's delicious, Tim," she said.

He was about to launch into a long, no doubt uncomfortable and boring monologue about how he had come to choose it, but Conrad Brittan, her dad—silver-haired and distinguished, wearing a suit that probably set him back the equivalent of a month of Tim's salary—interrupted him. "So, Jessica tells us you two met at the magazine?"

"Yes, sir," Tim said, grateful for the question.

"Are you in the art department with Jessica?" Chelsea asked.

Tim shook his head. "I'm an associate editor."

"That sounds very impressive," Arlene said. She was still eyeing Tim with an intensity that made him feel ill at ease. He'd been hoping Jessica could sneak into his room tonight, but suddenly feared that Arlene might show up instead.

"It's really just a glorified fact-checker," he said, trying to downplay the "impressive" thing. Not that a millionaire's wife would have any reason to be impressed by an associate editor, but at this point he wasn't about to try to build himself up into anything more than he was.

"Tim's very good at his job," Jessica offered helpfully.

Conrad Brittan, whose only "job" seemed to consist of managing his family's wealth, changed the subject again. Tim didn't mind; work was such a mundane topic in this rarefied atmosphere, and probably not suited to holiday conversation anyway.

But the area he changed it to was one that was even less comfortable for Tim.

"How about family?" Conrad asked him. "You got any family nearby? Any brothers? Sisters?"

"No, sir," Tim said flatly, hoping a less-than-enthusiastic response would prompt him to drop it. "No brothers or sisters. It's just me."

"How about your folks?"

Tim caught Jessica's eye and she gave a sympathetic smile. Before he could answer, Jessica's grandmother, who seemed to miss about a third of any given conversation, broke in. "Let the boy eat!" she commanded.

Conrad sighed and addressed her with the weary patience of someone who'd had this discussion many times before. "We're just talking, Mother."

"Dad—" Jessica started.

But Tim interrupted her, hoping to put a lid on the whole topic. "The family thing's kind of complicated, sir."

"Complicated?" Conrad asked. "How so?"

He clearly wasn't going to drop it easily. Now Arlene, also seemingly recognizing Tim's discomfiture, stepped in. She raised a forkful of the pistachio and apple stuffing that Jessica's sister had made. "This stuffing is delicious, Chelsea."

But Jessica had already gone into defensive mode, and she continued her statement. "Tim's always had kind of a strained relationship with his parents."

"Well, who hasn't?" Conrad asked with a wry smile. He refrained from glancing at his mother, but Tim noticed the old woman stiffening a little. She missed a lot, but she hadn't missed that line.

"Tim's father ran out when he was eight," Jessica

went on. Now she was carrying it farther than her dad probably would have, and Tim fervently wished she'd put on the brakes. She had an argumentative streak, Tim knew, and was probably just going on to give her dad a hard time for bringing it up at all. But Tim was the one who'd end up getting the worst of it.

"Jess . . ." he started.

"Oh, that's sad," Chelsea interrupted.

Jessica didn't miss a beat. "Then he had to go live with his uncle, in a tiny room in the back of his bar."

"Really?" Chelsea asked, wide-eyed.

"What about your mother?" Conrad asked.

And there it is, Timmy. Topic number one on the hit parade of issues you don't want to discuss at Thanksgiving dinner, especially with the girlfriend's parents. Tim glanced at Jessica, who was looking at him expectantly, along with everyone else at the table. No help there. "Uh, that . . . uh . . ." he stammered. How to phrase it? There was no good way, no easy out. "She sort of had a tough time . . . after my dad left." That was pretty nonspecific. Also sort of incomplete. It hadn't just been her, after all. "It was pretty hard on both of us."

Arlene dripped sympathy. "I'm sure."

Tim swallowed hard. Comparing this huge extended family to his own small, broken one was not unlike the feeling he'd had when he'd parked his shabby old Mustang next to the polished Bentley outside. Only with more emotional freight attached.

"Anything else you wanted to know, Dad?" Jessica asked, her point made.

An awkward silence followed. Tim would have

words with Jessica later, he was sure. Right now, though, he just wanted someone to move on, to put an end to his anguish.

Finally, it was Jessica's grandmother who piped up. "Would someone pass the sweet potatoes?"

The rest of the meal passed without incident, and after it was over, Tim collapsed in the family's media room with Jessica, her dad, Chelsea's husband, Brad, and the kids, and watched a football game on a TV nearly as large as Tim's front door. Dessert, coffee, and brandy were served in there, and even though Tim was pretty sure his stomach would explode, he couldn't turn down the pumpkin-ginger cheesecake after he got a whiff of it.

Finally, it was time to head upstairs for bed. Tim hadn't had a chance to get Jessica alone until they were on the grand staircase. He clutched her hand, holding it a little tighter than was absolutely necessary. "You have fun down there?" he asked, his anger abated only a little by the cheesecake and brandy.

"Oh, come on," she said, the very picture of intransigence. "They could use a little shaking up." Jessica gave him a sly grin. "Did you see my sister when I said you lived in a tiny room in the back of your uncle's bar?"

The trouble with Jessica was that he couldn't stay mad at her. She liked to stir up trouble, but there was a naïveté to the way she did it that was charming instead of obnoxious. At least, after the fact.

Way after.

"I had my own room, you know," he reminded her.

"I was just trying to make it a better story."

"Is that why you wanted me here? To freak out your family?"

They came to a stop outside the guest room where he'd tossed his bag earlier, and she turned to him, putting her hands on his chest, pushing close to him. "No. I'm sorry, okay? I didn't mean to get you upset." She lowered her voice, brought her face close to his ear. He could feel her hot breath when she spoke. "Tell you what . . . I have to go down and say goodnight to everyone, but I'll sneak in later and make it up to you, okay?"

Which was what Tim had been hoping for all along. Something about making love with her in her rich family's manse was terribly appealing. "In that case," he teased, "I'll put on something naughty." He pulled Jessica to him, kissed her deeply, tasting her, and then released her. She went back to the stairs and he opened the door to the room he had looked at only briefly before. Clicked on the overhead light.

It was a beautiful guest room. Antique bed with dust ruffle, marble-topped dresser, armoire, framed paintings on the walls, an obviously pricey Persian rug covering some of the hardwood floor. A bedside table held a lamp, a digital clock-radio, a couple of hardcover books, and some magazines.

A closet, its door standing slightly ajar.

A chill shook Tim. He gripped the jamb until the moment passed.

Forcing himself into the room, he switched on the bedside lamp. That was better, but the room was still full of shadows, dark pools where anything could be hiding. And that closet . . . he went over and pushed the door shut until it clicked firmly in place. Returned to the bed and tucked the dust ruffle underneath the mattress, so the bare floor beneath the bed was exposed. His overnight bag was on a cedar chest at the end of the bed. He would leave it there, to help hold the lid closed.

Tim felt uncomfortable here, fearful. Shadows everywhere. But there wasn't much he could do about it, short of leaving. And Jessica would go nuclear if he even thought about doing that.

He braved the hallway, went across to the bathroom, brushed his teeth. Back in the guest room, he went through the whole inspection procedure again. Nothing under the bed, closet door still closed, armoire tight. The cedar chest hadn't opened itself and spilled the contents of his overnight bag. Tim stripped down to a T-shirt and boxers, draped his discarded clothing over a chair, and sat down on the edge of the bed, steeling himself to turn off lights and try to sleep.

Then, remembering that his feet dangled before that big empty space under the bed (space that had been empty a moment ago, at least) he yanked them up, swung them onto the bed, stuffed them safely under the covers.

Old habits died hard.

Five

Okay, sleep wasn't happening.

The bedside lamp still burned in Tim's room. Even with its glow, he couldn't relax enough to let sleep overtake him. He was tense, on edge. Waiting for something to happen, even though he couldn't say what. The night before, after his walk home, he hadn't slept well. He should have been exhausted tonight.

But there were too many shadows here. . . .

He fought for sleep, knowing the whole time that the more he tried, the farther away it would remain. After a long stretch of time passed, the doorknob started to turn. He didn't want to be caught wide awake, half-panicked over nothing. He quickly turned off the light and dropped back down onto the mattress, feigning sleep. Breathing heavily, eyes closed. A moment later, he felt the pressure as Jessica climbed into the bed beside him without saying anything. He shifted, moving toward her warmth, her familiar weight. Wrapped an arm around her, spooning her. She smelled different, somehow—probably washed off the perfume from earlier, he guessed.

"I like this sneaking around thing," he murmured softly. He kissed the hair on the back of her head. "It's kinda sexy."

Jessica didn't answer, didn't respond. Her nightgown wasn't the slinky thing he had expected her to wear; it felt like rough cotton. "You all right?" he asked.

Still no answer. He moved closer to nuzzle her neck, kiss it. But her lack of responsiveness disturbed him. It wasn't like her. "Jess, what is it? Did something happ—"

With the lamp off, the only light in the room was that from the moon, streaming in through curtains Tim had left parted. But that was enough, when he really looked, to see that something was very wrong. He felt his stomach lurch.

Jessica's neck was a mass of wrinkles.

Old skin.

Her mom? Tim reached over her for the lamp, switched it on.

And jumped out of bed, away from what he saw, away from what couldn't possibly be. He landed on the floor, his back against the wall, staring up in horror.

She was in her fifties, but looked older. She didn't wear a nightgown at all, but a hospital gown, drab and shapeless. Her straw-blond hair hung in lifeless strings around her face. Wrinkled flesh sagged around weary eyes, lips cracked and caked with drool.

"Mom?"

It couldn't be. Tim's mother was nowhere near here. If she had shown up, someone would have told him, they wouldn't have let her just slip into his room. So it wasn't real, wasn't his mom, was just another hallucination in a string of them.

Only this was a bad one. *Really bad, Timmy, seeing things like this.*

Then she started to speak, or tried to. But her voice caught and she choked, started coughing. The huge, phlegmy coughs wracked her body, sounded like her lungs were trying to work their way out of her. Finally, blood spewed from her mouth, splattering on the bedspread.

When his mother brought her hacking under control, she smiled down at Tim, blood coating her teeth. Tim fought down his revulsion, but he knew his terror showed on his face. He couldn't get any farther away; the wall blocked his retreat.

She pushed the covers aside and climbed out of the bed. "Where are you going?" she asked. "Don't run away."

It was her voice, Tim knew. He recognized it, had known it all his life, and somehow that made things even worse. A visual hallucination he could deal with—hell, he was almost getting used to those. And those strange noises the night before, they were scary but somehow okay. But this . . . his own mother's voice, the voice that had always soothed, always comforted . . . he couldn't take it. He averted his eyes, looked at her feet, the skin cracked and bloody, nails yellow and jagged.

"Why won't you look at me?" she asked. She took a step toward him, then another. "Look at me, Tim." Not a question now, but a command. Even her pace picked up. There was nothing tentative about her movements now. Tim couldn't speak, couldn't scream. All he could do was sit on the floor in abject horror, wishing it would just go away.

His mother bent forward, put a cold hand on his face, the skin of her palm like sandpaper, dry and cracked. "Look . . . at . . . me."

Unbearable. He closed his eyes. "One, two, three . . ."

"Tim."

He ignored the voice, kept counting. Usually the counting dispelled the fear, but it wasn't, not this time. His breath came in wet shudders, and he continued, even louder now. "Four, five . . ."

"Tim?"

That sounded like Jessica, not his mother. He risked opening his eyes, afraid of what might be in front of him when he did. He was on the floor. The bed was a disaster, covers thrown back in a tangle. The closet door hung open. Jessica stood in the doorway wearing a sexy nightie and looking at him with obvious concern. "Tim, what are you doing on the floor?"

Tim blew out a breath, willing his heart rate to slow. His mother wasn't there; the blood she had sprayed around the room had vanished when she did. "God, I had the freakiest dream," he admitted when he could finally find his voice.

"What was it?"

"My mom." He remembered Uncle Mike's phone

call from the day before, and a sudden sense of urgency struck him. "I need to see her."

Jessica came fully into the room, closing the door behind her. She favored Tim with a seductive smile and ran her hands down the sides of her breasts, her waist, stopping at her hips. Tim felt arousal competing with the horror that had overwhelmed him just minutes before. "Get back in bed," she said, her voice husky now, a little breathless. "I'll make you forget all about your bad dreams."

Tim appreciated the promise of that statement, and he started to get up off the floor. He was still more than a little embarrassed at the way she had found him, but the blood stirred in him at the sight of her, the desire she always instilled in him forcing away all other thoughts.

Before he could reach the bed, though, his cell phone started to chirp insistently. Tim hesitated, disoriented. *Who would be calling so late?* he wondered. "Where's my phone?"

He started digging through his overnight bag, not finding it. The phone kept ringing. "Let it go to voice mail," Jessica suggested.

But that wasn't an option, if he could help it. No one would call him at this hour unless it was important, so he wanted to get it. Or else it was a wrong number, in which case he wanted the opportunity to yell at the caller. Finally, he turned it up, underneath the clothes he'd piled on the chair. Flicked it open. "Hello?"

Jessica dropped down on the bed, frowning, evidently unhappy at being upstaged by a phone call.

Tim tossed her an apologetic shrug and tried to ignore her.

It was his Uncle Mike on the phone. His voice was agitated, his words unclear, and Tim couldn't focus on what he was saying. "Hey, Uncle Mike. I got your message. Look, I'm heading over there to see Mom tomorrow—"

"I thought you were staying here this weekend," Jessica said, loud enough to drown out Uncle Mike's voice. Tim turned his back to her, trying to make out his uncle's words.

"What?" he asked, having missed something that sounded important. "What happened?"

His uncle repeated himself, and Tim felt his world falling apart.

Tim could hardly believe what he had heard—horrible enough by itself, but made even more so by the timing of his awful visitation. Massive heart failure, Uncle Mike called it. The home where she had been living for these past months had telephoned Uncle Mike earlier in the day to tell him that she wasn't doing well. But, he insisted, they hadn't told him just how bad she really was—probably had not even known themselves.

After that, according to what they'd told him, she had faded fast. They had brought around some Thanksgiving dinner, but she hadn't wanted to eat. Her mood had been sour. She had grouched at the attendants, waved away her neighbors. She had called for Rob—Tim's dad—who had been gone for so many years, and when he hadn't come she had complained bitterly.

Then she had gone quiet, watching TV, ignoring everyone else. Uncle Mike said she had gone to bed early. She had awakened a few hours later, calling out and clutching for the attendant call button beside her bed. By the time anyone made it into her room, she had fallen half out of bed. She was already gone by then, Uncle Mike said. The end had been fast and probably relatively painless.

Except Tim knew it wasn't as painless as he thought. Or else, that hadn't really been the end. Because about the time she had been dying in a nursing home a hundred miles away, she had also been paying an unexpected visit to her only son.

The world was a strange, often frightening place. That was a lesson he had learned early on in life. He guessed most kids did. But in his case, he kept having it reinforced, time and again. He was, by this time, more than a little tired of it. His earliest lessons, especially his father's disappearance, had sent him into psychiatric care, and had nearly destroyed his mother. Dr. Jane Matheson had, eventually, helped steer him away from madness. She had been very pragmatic, completely scientific. It was only years later, after he was out of her care, that he started to think maybe there really was more going on than rational science could explain.

Certainly, everything he had seen and experienced in the last couple of days could have been imaginary. Probably was, in fact.

But the appearance of his mother, at right around the

same time she had been dying, was just a little bit harder to accept. Well, a lot harder, really. Tim drove through the night, away from Jessica's parents house, toward Danville. He kept remembering his mom in the apparition, blood flecking her teeth like she was some kind of vampire, putting her sandpaper hand against his face.

That wasn't real, he told himself. That had just been some kind of nightmare, at best some sort of random electrical impulses generated by her death. Tim wasn't really up on theories of psychic phenomena, and studying them would have worked against his long effort to deny their reality, but he was sure there was one that would explain such a visitation in scientific, or pseudoscientific, terms.

Instead of dwelling on it, he tried to remember better times with Mom. Those had all been very long ago, and even they were tempered with the knowledge that Dad had been around then, as well. Almost any happy moment with Mom had carried the risk of becoming a moment of living hell, if he happened along and was in one of his customary nasty moods.

Still, there were snatches of time that he had tucked away, like a squirrel hoarding nuts against winter's cold. His mom reading Spider-Man comics to him one day when he'd stayed home from school, sick. She had acted them out, doing all the voices from Peter Parker's nebbishy weakling to Aunt May's doddering old lady to a gruff snarl for J. Jonah Jameson.

Or the time that they had gone to Virginia, for a reason he couldn't even remember now. It had been just the two of them. The old man had stayed behind.

They'd had a hotel room together, and she had let Tim order from room service and watch cartoons, and then in the morning they had played in the hotel pool.

When his dad had gone away for good, things had changed. He couldn't remember his mother ever really being happy again after that. Her smile had always seemed strained, like a beauty pageant loser's forced gaiety while congratulating the winner. She had tried, for a while.

Then she had stopped doing even that. That's when he'd gone to live with Uncle Mike. That's when, to Tim's mind, her long disintegration had begun. She had seemed ageless before that, as perfect and unchanging as a statue. But after that, every time he had seen her, she had added a new line, a new wrinkle, some gray hairs.

It was astonishing, in a way, that she had hung on as long as she did after the time that she seemed to have just given up on life. She had retreated into herself, participating only occasionally. She came to Tim's high school graduation, and when he got his degree from J-school, she had given him a briefcase. That had been the last time he could remember seeing her truly smiling, really engaged with the world around her.

Once again, he tried to push his thoughts away from the later years and back toward the happy times. Back to the days when his mother had been blond and lovely and cheerful, glowing like a bright star that had fallen to Earth but, instead of feeling trapped, loved it here and wanted to stay.

He fixed that image in his head, and kept driving.

Six

The Danville State Children's Institute was a drab, bureaucratic-looking place from the outside. Gray stone, windows trimmed in peeling white paint. The sky overhead seemed to mirror the color of its walls, glowering and leaden on an overcast afternoon.

Inside, though, attempts had been made to cheer the facility up as much as possible. Interior walls were painted in soothing pastels or bright, primary colors. Painted animals romped on their smooth surfaces, and even administrative necessities—plastic mailboxes outside office doors, for instance—were decorated with fun, colorful stickers or crafted to look like the faces of lions or bears.

As much as his old room at his parents' place, or the apartment behind Uncle Mike's bar that Jessica was so fond of bringing up to people, this place was Tim's boyhood home. He still recognized its hallways and public spaces. This was where he had learned the word "scotophobia." Afraid of the dark. Dr. Matheson had been a firm believer in the power of words, of ideas. "Name that which you are afraid of," she often said, "and it gives you a handle with which to control it."

For young Tim Jensen, that had been a very long list of names. Afraid of the dark, the night, shadows, closets.

Afraid, most of all, of the Boogeyman.

He had watched Dr. Matheson's kindly face with the utmost care, the first time he had dared to speak that name to her. He waited for a hint of a smile, a lifting of the brow, a twinkle in the eyes that would indicate how amusing she found his worst fear.

None of those things happened.

Dr. Matheson had held his gaze for a moment, nodded, then looked away to scribble another note on her pad. She had not said, "There's no such thing," or any of the other phrases he was used to adults tossing out every time he mentioned the dark man he claimed had taken his father away. She had simply accepted it, like it was just another one of his litany of fears, every bit as real as closets and shadows.

"Sciophobia," he remembered. Fear of shadows.

Eventually, of course, she had tried to persuade him that the Boogeyman didn't exist. She had to, he realized. She couldn't let him go on believing his dad had been snatched away by some mythical monster. That would be unprofessional, irresponsible, and Dr. Jane Matheson was neither of those.

"Parents tell their children horrible things some-times," she had explained. They had been in her office, she sitting in the leather chair beside her desk and he sprawled on the fluorescent purple beanbag she kept for her young charges. "They don't mean to frighten them, not really—mostly, they are just looking for a way to persuade their children that their actions have consequences. But when you're six or seven, do you think it's easy to understand that if you don't eat your vegetables, you may not get all the nutrients your body needs? Or is it easier to understand that if you don't eat your vegetables, some awful monster will come out from under your bed and get you?"

"The monster," Tim answered solemnly.

"That's what I think, too," Dr. Matheson said. "In the long run, it may not be the best idea. But at the mo-ment, a six-year-old may not care as much about get-ting proper nutrition as he does about not being eaten himself. Parents expect that, before belief in these monsters becomes a serious problem, their children will be old enough to realize that they are not real."

"And I'm old enough," Tim said.

"Yes, you are. But it's not always just a function of age, Tim. Sometimes other things get mixed in. In your case, it was your father, leaving you and your mother, while you were at that impressionable age. In your young mind, you couldn't understand why he would do that—couldn't even accept that someone *might* do that. So your mind had to substitute another explana-tion. And what it chose was what you feared the most—a Boogeyman, coming out of a dark closet, stole him away. It's perfectly understandable, and not as uncommon as you probably think."

Tim had brightened at that idea. "You mean, other kids believe in him too?"

Dr. Matheson nodded and tapped the end of her pen on her little notepad. "Parents around the world tell similar stories to their children, and sometimes the children believe it. Not just about Boogeymen but about vampires or werewolves or changelings—all kinds of strange and scary monsters."

"But those things aren't real," Tim said. "I've seen them in movies and *Scooby Doo* and stuff, but—" He stopped, comprehension dawning on him.

"That's right, Tim. Those things aren't real. And neither is the Boogeyman. He only lives in your mind. He's only something that we might call a construction, or a personification, of your fears. He does not really exist, and he cannot hurt you, ever."

Dr. Jane Matheson's hair had silvered during the time he had known her, lines had formed around her eyes and at the corners of her mouth, but her soft blue eyes hadn't changed and her manner still radiated calm wisdom. Her white lab coat looked new, and she wore it over a cheerful red pants suit. He felt better just being in her presence. She exuded a kind of centeredness that never failed to reassure him. As she walked through the art room with him, he watched kids working with crayons, clay, and water colors, and remembered when it had been him playing with those things.

"So the funeral's today?" she asked. She had a way of cutting right to the heart of things.

"Yeah, this afternoon."

"I'm so sorry." Her empathy, Tim had no doubt, was genuine. Dr. Matheson was one of the best people he had ever known, and he trusted her absolutely.

"Me too."

They watched a boy coloring in black eyes above a red house—chimney on top, smoke curling out of it. It reminded Tim of his childhood home—the house that had figured in so many of his conversations with Dr. Matheson. Arching an eyebrow at the picture, he figured she knew it, too. "I'm thinking of going by the old house," Tim said.

"Really?"

"My uncle's been fixing up the place since Mom went into the hospital last year," he explained, knowing even as he did so that it was hardly a sufficient explanation. One of Dr. Matheson's many gifts, though, was patience. She knew—had always known—that he'd tell her what was really going on with him when he was ready to.

Apparently satisfied with his masterpiece, the kid put down the crayon, regarded his work for a moment, then picked it up off the table and offered it to Tim.

"He wants you to have it," Dr. Matheson told him.

For a moment, he thought she was talking about his family's old house, saying that Uncle Mike wanted him to have the place. Then he realized she meant the picture, and he took it from the boy's hand. "Thanks," he said, smiling, genuinely touched by the offer.

The kid beamed and Dr. Matheson tousled his hair. Tim looked at the picture a moment longer, but realized that it kind of creeped him out. It was just a kid's idealized version of a house—door, four windows, that chimney. But the eyes, floating in the sky above it, were disturbing. He remembered the eyes he thought he'd seen in the back of the man's head, in the park the other night.

Dr. Matheson moved on, heading out the door and into the long hallway toward the front, and he followed. "I haven't been home since I was a little kid," he admitted. "I'm scared something horrible will happen the second I step in that house."

"Aren't the horrible things already happening?" she asked. "Your fears have disrupted your personal life, gotten in the way of your relationships. Tim, *something* happened in that house, but it wasn't supernatural. There's nothing in there but memories."

He tried to think of something to say in response, but nothing would come. Of course, she was right. She always was. And she always sounded so sensible when she spoke.

But she hadn't been there on Thanksgiving night, when his mom had "visited." Maybe that was all in his head, too, but the way her appearance had corresponded with her death . . . that couldn't be mere coincidence. There was more to it than that. It was in the dark, in the shadows, when Dr. Matheson wasn't around, that he most needed her calm rationality.

"You dealt with your father leaving the best way you could," she went on. "But you were eight. You're a grown man now. It's time to move on. These feelings you have are going to get worse and worse unless you face this. Come on, you've been coming here for, what ... fifteen years? Look around you. There are only children here, Tim."

She was right again. Tim knew that, knew he was too old to continue seeing a child psychologist. A little girl carried a red ball down the hallway, holding it close, as if it was a beloved stuffed animal. She smiled shyly at Dr. Matheson, looked away from Tim.

"I want to get better," Tim declared. "I want a normal life."

"Then you know what you have to do. You've always known."

Tim thought he knew what she meant, but he wanted her to say it. Needed her to. It wasn't an idea he could embrace easily, certainly not one he would volunteer without a little prodding. He stayed silent and let her spell it out.

"Go home, Tim. Spend one night in that house. Trust me, it's going to help."

There it is, Timmy. It's so simple, isn't it? At least, the way she says it.

Tim started to respond, but an electronic voice from an overhead speaker cut him off. "*Dr. Matheson to observation.*"

She put a hand on his arm. "I'm sorry," she said. "I've got to go." She started walking backward down the hall, still looking at him, her expression sincere, concerned. "Just one night, and you'll see. The only monster is the one you created in your mind."

Then she turned around and hurried away. The intercom crackled again, but Tim barely heard it. He was listening to an inner voice now.

Is that right, Timmy? Just in your mind? There's only one way to find out, isn't there? Are you really ready to grow up?

Tim stood alone in the quiet hallway for a moment, trying to steel himself to leave the place. He felt safe here—it was one of the few places outside of his own apartment where he did. He knew it was a strange perception to have of such a place. He had been drugged here, and physically restrained, especially in his earliest days, when Uncle Mike had realized he couldn't deal with Tim's panic attacks, when everyone had been afraid he'd hurt himself, or worse. He had been so lonely on those nights, away from anyone he had ever known or loved. He had felt like a castoff, a pariah, a prisoner. Thrown into this pit because no one wanted to love him or care for him, because even his own family members couldn't stand to have the crazy kid around.

It had taken a while to get over that, but he had. With Dr. Matheson's help, and then with the other kids in their group sessions, Tim had worked through those feelings of persecution, of being unwanted. He had come to realize that they had put him here *because* they loved him, because they wanted him to get better, and knew they had reached the limits of what they could do to help him.

His mom had come to visit him sometimes, but mostly Uncle Mike came. He explained that it was hard for her to see her son and not to be able to take him home. It made her cry, he said, made her so sad she could hardly bear it.

Tim always thought that maybe Uncle Mike was trying to put one over on him on that count. She had never had any problem leaving him at Uncle Mike's place on the days that the three of them did something together, or on those more rare occasions when she took him by herself for the day. Tim guessed it was seeing him in an institution that bothered her, more than having to go home alone.

In those days, he had never thought about how much it would hurt in another fifteen years when he had to visit her in a nursing home. Turning the tables, he had learned, didn't make things any easier.

Finally, his feet were willing to obey his head, and he started for the exit. But as he pulled even with a doorway, a piercing, terrified scream from within shattered the silence. Tim stopped short, looking in both directions for a nurse or orderly. Seeing no one nearby, he shoved through the door.

Inside, the room was a traditional hospital-type room except for the colorful cartoon character wallpaper. On the bed, a little girl thrashed wildly, her blankets flapping around her as if in a hurricane wind. Her blue eyes wouldn't settle on anything for more than a fraction of a second, but darted around madly. Tim had a quick flash of recognition, almost déjà vu, when he realized that he must have looked very much the same in his first days here.

"It's okay," Tim said, trying to soothe her. He was afraid to approach, though—the way she floundered made him worry that she would hurt herself, and his presence only seemed to make things worse. "It's okay," he repeated, over her screams. Then he stuck his head back out the door. "Hey! We need some help in here!"

The girl didn't stop flailing or screaming. Tim was certain she would suffer serious injury if someone didn't calm her down fast. At the back of her bed, he spotted the nurse call button, and he dashed over, squeezing it. Her tiny fists and feet lashed out toward him when he neared her, the violence of her motion somehow incongruous with her bunny rabbit pajamas. "Easy," he said. "The nurses will be right here, I promise. It's all right. It's all right."

For a second, he thought his words were having some impact. She stopped thrashing, went still—but her gaze was fixed on something over Tim's shoulder, fear still etched on her pretty young face. "What?" Tim asked her. "What is it?"

She gave no answer. She had stopped screaming, but her mouth hung open, chin slack, a line of saliva trailing from her lips. Tim looked over his shoulder at walls, cartoon characters. "There's nothing there."

But even as he spoke, a sound moved behind him, like a rat's little claws—up the far wall, across the ceiling, stopping, finally, at a spot where one of the overhead acoustical tiles was loose.

And there was a dark, shadowed gap in the ceiling.

From the shadows, a pair of tiny eyes glared down at him.

Tim glanced back at the little girl, who was shivering now, shaking uncontrollably, spittle flying in every direction from her open mouth. Before he could move toward her again, nurses rushed into the room, shoving him aside.

"I was . . . she was screaming," he tried to explain. "There was something in—"

No one was listening to him. "Prepare a syringe!" one of the nurses shouted. "She's having a seizure! Someone help me hold her down!"

Other nurses and orderlies crowded around. Tim saw one push a bite plate into the girl's mouth while others tugged on long nylon straps, fastening them beneath her, tying her down on the bed. A needle appeared in the first nurse's beefy hand and she drove it into the little girl's flesh. Tim hated needles, had to look away.

Instead of looking down, though, or to the side, he felt his gaze drifting inexorably up. At the ceiling, the gap in the tiles. Nothing there, now. If there ever had been.

He looked back at the girl again, locking eyes with her. Already, her shuddering was starting to come under control, but her eyes still showed the fear she had known. She held Tim's gaze. She couldn't speak, but her eyes seemed to communicate for her. *I saw it too,* they said. *We both saw the same thing. . . .*

Seven

The funeral home had once been the grandest building on a block of impressive structures, with its Doric columns, its Greek Revival façade, its stately air. But the neighborhood around it had become depressed, gone downhill. The bank that had once commanded the corner had been knocked down a decade before, and a strip mall had taken its place. Half of that mall's storefronts were empty now, boarded over. The remaining ones held a laundromat, an Asian restaurant, a video store. Between there and the funeral home was a pawnshop and a bar, a scummy joint with a couple of motorcycles parked in front and a cardboard sign on the door that gave its hours of business, 6 A.M.–2 A.M., in bright orange letters. On a rainy day, with thunder rolling overhead and lightning flaring through the clouds, the block was an especially dreary place to be. Only one thing would draw Tim into this neighborhood.

And that one thing had happened. Mary Ellen Jensen had finally succumbed. The world had, Tim believed, had it in for his mother for a long time. That she held out as long as she did had been an amazing accomplishment, an act of will. Or else it was a giant middle finger raised to the forces that battered her, the fates that gave her the old man, Tim's dad, for a husband—small-minded, bullying, uninterested in anyone's happiness but his own—and that took him away so suddenly and mysteriously, that made Tim withdraw into himself and his nightmares, that finally snatched away his mother's health and sanity too.

Inside, the place had a sickly sweet aroma, as if all the flowers around were slowly rotting in their vases. Tim had met the funeral director—a thin, myopic ferret of a man in an appropriately black suit—had shaken hands with a couple of people, hugged Uncle Mike. Now he was alone in the viewing room, approaching her for the first time. Her casket was simple, your basic mahogany box. The open lid showed red velvet lining.

Part of him didn't want to look—wanted, in fact, to turn and run from here as fast as he possibly could. Funerals were not for the dead, he knew, but for the living, services to help people cope with their grief. Well, he had seen precious little of his mom since he'd been ten years old. He loved her, but the idea that he had lost someone he hadn't even had in the first place seemed a little silly. He didn't need the funeral, and he didn't want to be reminded that she had died all by herself in a nursing home, brought down by her own addictions, while he slept (well, tried to sleep) in luxury at the Brittan house.

He knew he couldn't leave, though. And he knew that if he didn't look at her, he would forever remember the apparition at Jessica's parents' place, and he didn't want that to be his last image of his mom. He walked slowly toward the casket, gaze on the threadbare carpet, the yellowed walls, his own black dress shoes, polished to a high gloss.

Finally, he stood before it and made himself look, half fearing that he would see her as she had appeared the other night, filthy and frightening. Instead, she was beautiful. Her hair had been styled, her face made up nicely, her hands crossed over her chest. She might have been catching a quick nap before going to a party. But this nap would last forever, and the party would never begin.

Tim tried once again to call up more memories of happier times, to remember who Mary Jensen had been in her prime. A Fourth of July block party, when she had been resplendent in a red blouse and blue skirt, with white pearls, shoes, and belt, handing out sparklers to the neighborhood kids. A quiet summer's day when he was playing outside by himself, as he had often done, being a shy and often fearful kid, and she brought him a glass of lemonade, then sat with him, asking interested questions about his army men. A winter afternoon, with howling winds buffeting the house when she made hot chocolate for him and the neighbor girl, Katie. The three of them had assembled puzzles together, and his mom's good spirits and natural charm had made the afternoon rush by. Nights, so many of them, when she tucked him in with a kiss and a story.

You can't sum up a lifetime standing here, Timmy, the voice said. *Good and bad, happy and sad—the memories will be with you forever. Just say your good-byes. There's a funeral waiting for you.*

He touched the edge of the casket once, and turned away.

The rain broke for the funeral, but the cemetery was dotted with puddles, the headstones still dark and slick with water. Colors seemed brighter, more saturated under the overcast sky than they would have on a sunny day, when the light would have washed them out. Green and orange lichens on some of the older stones seemed almost to glow, and a scrap of red plastic around the neck of a vase of white flowers fluttered, mesmerizing Tim's attention. Autumn leaves crusted the green grass, as if in imitation of the lichens Tim saw.

A couple of dozen people showed, many of whom Tim didn't even recognize. One person who should have been here but wasn't—assuming he had just abandoned them, like everyone said—was his father. Rob Jensen. He wondered briefly if any new attempt had been made to track him down, to let him know that the woman he had left behind had finally given up the fight. Probably not, he guessed. No one had been able to find him fifteen years before, and it would only be more difficult for anyone to do so now.

The other person who should have been there was Jessica. Given their last conversation, though, Tim hadn't even told her when or where the funeral was taking place. If she cared, she knew his cell number.

Everyone who was there wore dark clothes, of course, and several carried umbrellas in case the skies opened up once again. Tim and Uncle Mike were among the pallbearers, and Tim was surprised at how light the big box was, as if she weren't even inside.

Uncle Mike looked uncomfortable in his black suit. He wasn't a guy who ever wore formal clothes; Tim couldn't even remember the last time he'd worn a necktie. He was a blue collar man all the way, a working man who related to the working men who drank in his place because he was just like them. He could talk cars, construction, or sports with anyone who walked through his door, but he'd have been absolutely lost at *End Magazine*. Tim, more or less through osmosis, had learned how to mix drinks, though, and was often pressed into bartending service at parties. Uncle Mike's dark, thinning hair was starting to gray, Tim noticed. His craggy face was dour, his lips pressed together in a thin line, his hands loose at his sides, as he listened to the preacher's spiel.

"Thou knowest the secrets of our hearts," the pastor said. He was as gray as the sky—gray hair, gray pallor to his skin. His suit was black, but if it hadn't been he would have blended right into the background. He'd given a short service back at the funeral home, his words a series of platitudes that meant nothing except that he had never known Tim's mother for a day of her life. He had seemed genuine when he expressed his sorrow to Tim privately, but Tim figured that, like a stage actor mouthing the same lines day after day, they became second nature and not hard to sell. "Shut not thy merciful ears to our prayer, but spare us and suffer us not at our last hour. Dust thou art, and unto dust thou shalt return."

Tim found his mind wandering as the preacher droned on. He knew the words were important to some, but to him they were mostly just background noise. They wouldn't bring his mom back or make her life—or death—any more meaningful.

It might have helped, he thought, if Jessica had been here. As it stood, he had not only lost his mother, but possibly his girlfriend. When he had thrown his belongings into his overnight bag at her house on Thanksgiving night, she had been fuming. "What am I going to tell my parents?" she demanded. "That you just got up and left in the middle of the night?"

"You could tell them my mother died," Tim had replied.

"But—it's not like there's anything you can do for her now," she shot back, fury animating her eyes. "Your uncle is handling things, right?"

"Yeah . . ."

"So what can you do tonight? You haven't had enough sleep, you can't drive all that way in the middle of the night for nothing."

"Look, Jessica . . ." To really explain how he felt, why

he had to leave right now, he'd have had to tell her all about the visitation he'd had. She thought it was simply a bad dream, but he knew it was more than that, and the timing seemed to confirm it. He had to get out of here, couldn't spend another minute in this house, and she would just have to deal.

"Whatever, Tim. If you want to go dashing off into the night, go ahead. I can't stop you. I'll just tell my parents you flaked out, I guess."

"Yeah," Tim said, a burst of anger charging through him. She just didn't seem to get that his mother had died and that it meant something to him. His bag packed, they embraced tentatively, awkwardly, and then he ran out of the house. That was the last he'd seen her, or heard from her.

Looking off across the cemetery, yet another flash of color caught his eye. He watched for it again, and saw a young girl, standing in the shade of a tree. She wasn't part of the funeral, and this was the only one taking place here at the moment. She was just someone who had wandered into the cemetery. She was maybe eleven, and her clothes were oddly mismatched, as if she had dressed herself from thrift shop castoffs. Around her neck she had a striped, multicolored scarf. Beneath that, a red sweater with a white pattern arcing across her shoulders, like something out of *Heidi*. The sweater was zipped tight, but a dress trailed out from underneath it, and under the dress were blue jeans, and finally red sneakers. It was almost as if she had intentionally decided to wear every color not normally seen at funerals. Her hair was long, copper-colored, her face serious. She held Tim's gaze for a long time, until he decided he really should be paying attention to his mother's send-off.

Obviously, he had missed something. Uncle Mike nudged him. "You're supposed to throw some dirt in the hole," he whispered. "Nobody else can until you do."

He had been told about this part, but the cue had flown right past him. He squatted down, took a handful of earth, and tossed it gently onto his mother's casket. It rattled down on her, and for a brief moment he had the absurd hope that it wouldn't wake her up.

When the service was all over and the guests were dispersing, Tim walked out with Uncle Mike. His hand hurt from being squeezed so hard by so many people. "Thanks for doing all this," he said. His uncle had done all the planning, all the organizing—Tim wouldn't have known where to begin. Tim had been staying with Uncle Mike for the last few days, but had spent a lot of his time alone in his old room behind the bar, and making that trip to Danville to see Dr. Matheson. He didn't know how the man had arranged all this so quickly. Some people spent a year or more planning a wedding, Tim knew, and these days, it seemed that most of them had two or three of those during the course of a lifetime. Nobody ever got more than the one funeral, and it had to be cobbled together in less than a week.

"She was my sister."

Tim had no answer for that. Maybe it did explain enough—Tim, an only child, a fatherless boy, now an orphan, had never had a sibling so he didn't know.

Both men kept walking, hands in their pockets, back toward the cars parked on the curved gravel drive. "You heading back tonight?" Uncle Mike asked.

Tim had been stalling about this, not making a commitment to anyone but himself. Not even to Dr. Matheson, really. Now, it seemed, the time had come. He had to either say something, or give it up forever. "Actually, I was thinking I might stay around tonight. In the house."

Uncle Mike shot him a surprised glance. "I thought you didn't like being in that house."

"Yeah, well . . . it's just a house." He didn't want to go into detail—didn't want to have to tell his uncle, any more than he had wanted to tell Jessica, about the visitation the other night that had driven him back to Dr. Matheson. Uncle Mike knew he'd gone to see the psychiatrist, but not, in any detail, what they had talked about. He didn't know that she had pushed Tim to spend one night there.

Or that Tim had agreed, finally, that it was necessary.

It's just a house. If he said it, thought it, often enough, maybe it would be true.

"The place is a mess," Uncle Mike said, as if he was trying to talk Tim out of staying. "I've been doing a lot of work there, and . . . I got some people coming to look at it."

"I won't mess anything up." He didn't want to be dissuaded, now that he had made up his mind. It wouldn't take much to make him abandon his plan, but if he didn't do it now, especially because Uncle

Mike was planning to sell the place, then he never would. Once it was sold, it would be too late. He could just see showing up when the new owners were sitting down to dinner, and asking if he could spend the night to see if the Boogeyman was real.

Back into an institution, if that happened. Probably to stay.

Anyway, if Dr. Matheson was right—and she usually was—this was what he needed. If he never had another opportunity to spend the night in his boyhood home, he would never get well. Never silence the voice in his head, or escape the things that he saw.

Before Uncle Mike could answer, Tim spotted a young woman he hadn't noticed during the service. She was striking, with shoulder length brown hair, piercing blue eyes, and a jaw that would have made a sculptor proud. She pushed an older man in a wheel-chair, and even through her black funeral attire Tim could tell she was strong and fit.

"Is that Katie Houghton?" he asked. Tim recognized her father first, even though the man had been hale when he'd last seen him, and then deduced that the woman with him must be Katie. Her dad had changed a lot less in fifteen years than she had. She had grown up, and very nicely.

Uncle Mike followed Tim's gaze. "Yeah," he replied. "How long's it been?"

"A long time."

"Her father's gone downhill," Uncle Mike told him. "You should go say hi to them while you're here."

Tim had done enough socializing for one day. He

was tired, wrung out. He and Katie had been fast friends when they'd been little kids, but he couldn't face renewing the acquaintance right now. "Maybe I can stop by tomorrow," he suggested.

"She'd like that."

Tim and Uncle Mike had come in separate vehicles—Uncle Mike in an old, faded red pickup truck, Tim in his blue Mustang. They had reached the truck now, and Tim searched for something to say . . . ideally, something cogent or helpful in some way. The kind of wisdom people should share at funerals, to help others feel better. But his mind was blank.

Uncle Mike broke the silence. "You might want to sleep in your old room. It's the only one I haven't torn up yet."

"Thanks," Tim managed. That was good, he decided. "Thanks" covered a lot of territory. "Thanks for everything." The two men embraced stiffly, and then Tim started for his Mustang.

"Wait," Uncle Mike called after him.

Tim turned back toward his uncle. The older man fished in his pocket, pulled out a key ring with a couple of keys dangling from it. "You're not going to get into the place without these."

Tim smiled, nodded, took the keys from Uncle Mike's outstretched hand. As he did, Uncle Mike said, "It's been good seeing you again, Tim." He climbed into the truck, closed the door, and started the ignition. Tim stood on the side of the road and watched the man who had raised him drive off into the gloom.

Eight

The Monday after Thanksgiving, Jessica drove into work trying to shake the feeling that she'd forgotten something. She hadn't, she was pretty sure. She had a regular routine, a mental checklist. Wallet, keys, cell phone, teeth brushed, hair brushed, lip gloss, and out the door she went.

It wasn't until she rode up on the elevator that she realized what was nagging at her. She hadn't forgotten anything. But she hadn't talked to Tim last night—the first Sunday night in a long time that had happened. Everyone at the magazine knew they were together, so they didn't try to hide their relationship. But Tim liked to sleep in his own place, and the sterility of it drove her a little nuts. So most nights they slept alone, even if they had been together earlier, and they made a habit of phoning each other to say good night before they went to bed.

That call hadn't happened for the last few nights. Friday and Saturday, it hadn't seemed so strange to her, because she was still at her parents' house. But last night she had been back at her own apartment, slipping back into the routine. And Tim hadn't called. Nor had she called him; she wasn't even sure where he was.

So it was that break in the routine that troubled her, not actually forgetting anything. Strange as it sounded, that made her feel a little better.

She had thought she would kill Tim, that Thanksgiving night. Yes, his mother had passed away, and she didn't want to come across as some kind of ogre, but the fact was he hadn't lived with the woman since he was ten years old. He hardly ever saw her or even spoke to her. She had lived in a nursing home for some time—as long as Jessica had been going out with Tim, anyway. It was undeniably sad that she was gone, and Jessica felt sorry for Tim, but the fact remained that it was a little too late for the rushing-to-her-side bit.

So why take off in the middle of the night, in a way guaranteed to make her parents think she had brought home a man who was egocentric, rude, and quite possibly mentally unbalanced?

As it turned out, that was more or less exactly what they had thought. At breakfast the next morning, Jessica had showed up alone and had to explain Tim's absence. Her mother's eyes had welled up instantly, but then, empathy had always been her forte. "The poor dear," she said. "He seems like a very nice young man."

But Jessica's father, as usual, cut right to the heart of things. "Now, let me get this straight," he said. "This phone call said that she was dying?"

"No," Jessica replied softly. "That she was dead. She had died a little while before. The nursing home called Tim's uncle when they couldn't revive her, and then he called Tim here."

"So what did he think he could accomplish in the middle of the night?"

"I think he just wanted to be there. With his uncle."

"That's a reasonable thing, Conrad," her mom said with a sniffle.

"I should think he could have waited until morning," her dad argued. "Driving in the middle of the night like that, he's just as likely to kill himself or someone else trying to get there. Not to mention the bad manners it shows, taking off and leaving without so much as a thank-you or good-bye to your hosts."

"He was upset," Jessica pleaded. "He wasn't thinking straight. His mom was dead, you know? He just wanted to be doing something, I think."

"Endangering himself and others, more like it," her father groused. "Plain irresponsible."

Jessica had decided that there was no use arguing about it. Her mother was teary-eyed, probably because she wouldn't get the chance to flirt with Tim over omelets like she'd hoped to, and her dad had already made up his mind—had begun to at Thanksgiving dinner, in fact, when Jessica had goaded Tim into talking about his off-beat upbringing—that her boyfriend was a nut.

The rest of her time at her parents' home had been a little strained as a result. Jessica's sister, Chelsea, in particular, took delight in needling her about her missing boyfriend at every possible opportunity. Even Brad, Chelsea's husband, finally told his wife to stop picking on Jessica. To escape their criticism, and what was even worse, their pity, Jessica took to spending more time in her room, or watching old movies on TV, dodging the rest of the clan.

No wonder she wasn't in the best of moods this morning. The high of the holiday had been shattered. Normally she would have thought of Thanksgiving as the start of the Christmas holiday season, a time of building excitement, shopping and planning and baking, all culminating in a year-end festival of warmth and joy. This year, Tim's crisis had derailed that. She was sure she could get the train back on the tracks in a week or two, but it wouldn't be the same.

And as she walked through the offices, she wasn't sure if she'd be celebrating with him or without him this year. He hadn't called, hadn't been in touch at all since the night he had left. Maybe she should have tried his cell phone, but she thought that since he was the one who had left without notice, he was the one who needed to apologize. The more time passed without a call from him, the angrier she became that he wasn't calling, and the more determined that *she* would not call *him*.

Stupid, she knew. But who doesn't do stupid things from time to time?

After settling into her own desk and reading the numerous e-mails that had piled up over the long weekend, she decided she needed to go see Colson Temple, Tim's boss. With everything that had been going on, it was unlikely that Tim had bothered to call him, and with the next issue's deadlines fast approaching, he would wonder where his associate editor was.

Colson's office was a mess, as was the man himself. His desk was piled high with papers, file folders, CDs, books, and magazines—both *End* and a wide variety of others. Colson was a voracious reader, everyone said. He consumed words the way some people consumed coffee, or chocolate, or crack. His appetite for language was closely mirrored, judging from his size, by his taste for food. His desk was disheveled and unkempt, as was his person. He must have weighed in at a little more than three hundred pounds. His white shirts could have been sewn by tentmakers, and the ties he insisted on wearing with them seemed miniature by contrast, barely reaching halfway down the massive expanse of his front. His hair looked like it hadn't seen a comb or brush in years, but straggled from his head like escapees during a prison break, diving in every direction at once. He wore thick glasses that might never have met a cleaning cloth. Jessica wondered how he could even see to read.

She knocked on his door and he looked up from the sheaf of papers in his hands. "Hi, Jessica," he said pleasantly. "Have a good Thanksgiving?"

"Yes, thanks, Colson." She paused, suddenly not sure how to bring the topic up.

"Something I can do for you?"

"I was wondering if you'd heard from Tim."

"Jensen?" he asked. "No, and I'm a little upset about it. Crunch time, you know."

"I know," Jessica assured him. "You might not, though. Hear from Tim, I mean. His mother passed away over the weekend, and he had to go home for her funeral and everything. I was afraid that, with all the commotion, he might forget to let you know."

Colson's forehead wrinkled and his lips turned down. "I'm really sorry to hear that. You're not going?"

At first, Jessica didn't understand what he meant. "I'm sorry?"

"To the funeral."

"I . . . no. Tim . . . he's kind of private about family stuff, and everything. I've never even met her. And we thought it would be better if I stayed here. Plus, you know, deadlines, right?"

Colson smiled at that. The way he regarded her from behind those thick, smudged glasses made her think he was going to ask more questions. But then, she remembered, he was a journalist, and that's what they did.

He refrained, though. He smiled and nodded knowingly. "Deadlines, right. I appreciate you being here. It's got to be a hard time, for both of you. You and Tim have my deepest condolences."

"Thanks, Colson. When Tim calls me, I'll make sure he talks to you."

An easy promise to make, Jessica thought. Maybe a hard one to keep, though, because it presupposed that Tim would in fact call her. She excused herself and went back to her desk, still wishing for that new computer that would make meeting her deadlines less of a challenge.

* * *

The old house was surrounded by miles of brown, denuded farmland, already harvested at this time of year, sitting and waiting for the new planting and the spring. Tim hadn't been out this way in a long time, but the road was familiar to him as he drove it, less like real life than something from a movie he'd seen several times. He recognized a barn that drooped in the middle like a broken-down old nag, the rust stains on mailboxes and irrigation pipes, the blue farmhouse with yellow shutters that squatted right next to the road. Tim played the radio softly as he drove. He felt almost relaxed for the first time since Thanksgiving.

Sitting on the passenger seat was the key ring Uncle Mike had given him. It occurred to him that he had never before had keys to the place—when he had lived there with his folks, he'd been too young. Since he had moved away, there had been no reason to have any. Uncle Mike had taken care of the place for his mom, not that she had been able to live there for awhile. But now—

A black *something* dove right toward his windshield, startling Tim out of his reflections.

Tim stomped on the brake. Tires squealed on the blacktop, the car starting to fishtail on the country lane, but it was all too late. Whatever it was slammed into the glass. The windshield shattered but held in place, a spider web of fractures. Tim turned into the skid, correcting, starting to get back on course, but a truck's air horn blared at him, surprising him all over again. Through the broken glass he could see that he was in the middle of the narrow road, and the semi barreling down on him couldn't get around. Tim braked once more, pulling hard on the wheel, trying to get back into his own lane.

The truck boomed past, and Tim pulled over to the dirt shoulder, stopping in a cloud of dust. In a nearby field, horses whinnied and ran away from the car, no doubt horrified by all the noise on the previously quiet country lane. Tim was shaking, his mouth dry, his mind emptied of everything but terror. His heart pounded in his chest like he'd swallowed one of those horses and it was frantically beating its hooves against him from the inside, trying to get out.

Finally he was able to look up and through the glass, where he saw what had started the whole chain of events. A huge black crow was almost flattened against the shattered glass, a mass of bloody feathers, with one round, beady eye staring in at him. He thought he would retch, but swallowed a couple of times and fought it back.

He sat in the car for another minute, afraid that if he got out, his legs would refuse to support his weight and drop him into the road. Realizing he couldn't go anywhere with the bird on his windshield, though, he eventually forced himself from the car.

There was no other traffic. With his engine off, the only sound now was the ticking of his car and the distant whickering of the horses, who had stopped up on the hill and watched him. Tim found a stick by the side of the road and tried to pry the sticky black mass off his windshield with it.

He remembered reading somewhere that crows were very intelligent birds—smart enough to drop nuts under the wheels of moving cars, and then to keep out of the way until they could come back for the insides, opened by the cars' wheels. Maybe this one had been trying to do that, but its timing had been a little off. Now it was meat—red goo and black feathers, pasted to glass. Scraping at it, poking the persistent bits of matter that refused to let go, made Tim feel sick.

When he had as much off as he could, he got back in behind the wheel, cranked the engine, and turned on the spray and wipers. Water splashed in the filigree of cracked glass, then turned red, and the wiper smeared the bloody cocktail across his entire field of view.

Tim shrugged. Nothing more he could do about it right now. He checked the rear-view mirror and pulled back out onto the peaceful road. Squinting through red, feathered muck, he drove the rest of the way to the old family home. *Just think of it as rose-colored glasses,* he heard in his head. *Everything's right with the world through those, isn't it?*

Soon, the old house loomed ahead, separating from the gray sky at his approach. Tim pulled off the road onto the rutted, weed-tangled driveway. The familiar mailbox was so black with age and mold it looked like it had survived a fire. He didn't think it had—his mom or Uncle Mike would have said something if that had happened. A fence that had once surrounded the property was mostly gone, knocked down or carried away or simply disintegrated with age. The yard had grown wild—whatever Uncle Mike had been doing to the place didn't include gardening, apparently.

But the house itself looked like it did in Tim's memory. It was a Gothic Revival structure, with white walls, steeply pitched dark gray roofs broken by dormers, and white, curvilinear trim around the eaves and gable edges. A front porch with its own roof and trim wrapped around two walls. A couple of red brick chimneys topped the house. A fine house, in its day, and one of the neighborhood's standouts. It had been built originally by someone with serious money. By the time Tim's folks had bought it, it had fallen into disrepair. Tim's dad had tried to fix it up, but he'd been handier in his own mind than in reality, and while he had improved it, he had never gotten it back into prime condition.

Then, of course, he had vanished. Tim's mom had never done anything to the house after that, and it had degraded fast.

Tim had conflicting feelings about the place. On the one hand, he had lived here as a kid, had grown up here to some extent. Even though not all his childhood memories were happy ones, there were certainly some that qualified, and this house—and the surrounding countryside, where he'd hiked and run, fired BB guns, seen rabbits and foxes and opossum—was part of them. On the other hand, if he had been driving around looking for a house that looked haunted, this would have been the one he would have stopped at.

He climbed from the blood-caked car and regarded the place. Took a deep breath, blew it out.

It *was* haunted. There was no denying that. The place held memories Tim was afraid to face, images that had fed his nightmares ever since. This was the place that had stolen his sanity, taken his youth, shaped the rest of his life. When he really thought about why he had turned to journalism as a career, it came back to this house, to what had happened here. No one on Earth had believed Tim's story of his dad's disappearance. Tim's response to that disbelief, after the years of therapy that had ensued, had been to find a career where people did believe—where the whole point of the job was that he wasn't making up stories, but reporting what had really taken place. Shaping facts into a coherent story so that people would have no choice but to believe them.

So yeah, it was a haunted house. Its effects had carried over into every aspect of Tim's life.

And now, if Dr. Matheson was right, he had to face the house again. Had to go inside, to spend the night there. He had to confront his fears—the ghosts that had chased him from it in the first place.

Maybe the night of his mother's funeral wasn't the best time to do it.

If I can do it tonight. he thought, *I can beat it. I know I can.*

You just keep thinking that, Timmy. Be brave, that's a good boy. That'll take you far, just you wait and see. Just you wait, Timmy.

He pushed the voice away, determined to ignore it. *You're going into a box,* he told the voice, *and the box will be put into another box and dropped into that deep ocean inside my head where forgotten things go.*

After tonight, I won't be hearing from you any more.

He took another breath, held it for a second, and approached the front door, carrying the keys Uncle Mike had given him.

Nine

Uncle Mike had, indeed, been tearing the place up.
Tim stopped just inside the open door. At first,
the place had been pitch black, immersed in
shadow, and Tim had stiffened, almost turned around
and gone straight back to the car, back to the city. But
he found the light switch just inside, where he remembered, and flicked it on with trembling fingers. Illumination from a chandelier fixture bathed the room, and
he breathed a little easier.

Semitransparent plastic sheeting hung all over the
place, some of it spattered with paint or sawdust. Sections of wall had been torn away, exposing studs and
beams. Enough tools, paint cans, and containers of
nails to fill a hardware store were strewn around, almost haphazardly. For just a second Tim had a vision
of his uncle as some kind of madman, tearing the place

down little by little with no plan, no design, but as he examined the house further he realized that progress was being made. It was just slow, Uncle Mike working alone on a job that should have taken a team, and doing it around his schedule at the bar.

A breeze sighed through the place, rattling the plastic sheeting. Tim jumped, startled, and closed the open door behind him.

He was inside.

Whatever was going to happen would happen now.

The living room had a fireplace in its center, around which people had gathered on winter nights when his parents had both been around. Hot toddies, eggnog, and hot chocolate were consumed; jokes told; neighbors gossiped about, all sitting near its toasty blaze. Now it had been torn apart, dismantled. The brick base still stood in its usual spot, but some of the copper chimney was gone, a section sticking down from the ceiling its only remnant. An old cabinet TV stood in a corner with a plastic sheet draped over it, the big leather chair that had been known as "Dad's chair" still lorded over its usual corner, but the floor lamp that had stood behind it was gone.

On the floor, off by itself, sat a big cardboard box. Curious, Tim went to it, pried open its flaps, and sat down next to it. It looked as if Uncle Mike had been tossing stuff into it willy-nilly as he came across it. Tim found his mom's prized silverware wrapped in velvet, next to some everyday dinner dishes that were chipped and cracked. They rested unevenly on a surface that shifted every time Tim lifted something off. He dug down to find out what was in the bottom of the big box, and found photographs. Lots of them—loose, in shoeboxes, in an old leather album.

Crossing his legs on the floor, Tim brought the album onto his lap and thumbed through it. Family pictures, mostly. Vacations at the beach—Tim and his dad, shirtless, "making muscles" while they squinted into the sun. Mom's shadow lay across them, elbows out, holding the camera steady. She had never been a great photographer, but she had enjoyed capturing what moments she could.

He found another picture of himself as a small boy, bundled up against the cold in a coat, galoshes, and snow hat. He looked like a miniature version of the Michelin man, roly-poly and virtually immobile. Next to him, equally constrained, was a little girl with long dark hair. Their arms were wrapped over each other's shoulders, and both had broad smiles on their faces. Was it Kate? he wondered. He freed the photo from a couple of the corners that held it in place, turned it over. "Tim and Katie" was written on the back. Tim smiled, not remembering the exact moment, but enjoying the memories that it did bring up. He and Katie had been best pals in those days. He remembered having seen her at the funeral earlier. He really would have to make a point of visiting her while he was in the neighborhood.

Another photo caught his eye a couple of pages later. Taken by someone else, maybe Uncle Mike or some family friend, it showed Mom and Dad, both looking much younger, happy, in love. They sat together on a sofa, leaning in toward each other, Dad's muscular arm thrown across Mom's shoulders. On Dad's knee, facing the camera with a quizzical expression, was a tiny tyke who could only be baby Tim. Everyone smiled, except little Tim. The scene was practically idyllic.

But that was so long ago. The picture was fading with the years, just like the memory of those happier, more innocent days had largely faded from Tim's memory. He tried to bring them back, wanted to remember when things had been good, and—

A whirring noise, electric, emanated from the kitchen. Some kind of appliance or power tool, Tim guessed. Uncle Mike wasn't here working, though. Maybe he had a helper after all. That would be a good thing, considering how much needed to be done. "Hello?" Tim called. He put the album back in the box, pushed to his feet.

His funeral pants were dusted white from the plaster he'd been sitting in. He batted at them as he walked into the dining room. A sheet of paint-smeared plastic hung in the doorway that separated the living room from the kitchen, but through it he could see a vague outline moving around in there, its shape distorted by the plastic.

He hoped.

He remembered the shadow man from the park, his own form misshapen and strange. This person didn't look quite like that had—but he or she didn't look completely dissimilar, either, much to Tim's dismay.

And that noise, the whirring sound, was familiar

somehow. "Hello?" he asked again, but there was still no response, just that continued noise.

But then he heard a voice call his name—soft, feminine, a voice that he knew well, and that couldn't possibly be calling him. He swallowed, braced himself, pushing the plastic aside with a quaking hand.

His mom stood at the counter—blonde and pretty, as he liked to remember her. In her mid-thirties, he guessed, wearing a pink shirt with polka dots, and soft jeans. She watched as a can of cat food rotated on the electric can opener, whirring until it had completed its circuit. When it was done, she forked some of the food into the cat's red supper dish. Lulu, their chubby calico, waited beside the dish, and she dove into the meal as soon as Mom put the dish down on the floor. Mom gave Tim a stern look, but there was still a bit of a smile in her eyes. "Tim," she said, "it's your cat. You're supposed to feed her."

Tim was about to answer—he'd been planning to feed her, but his math homework had taken longer than expected—but his dad's voice boomed from the back hallway, drowning him out. "I can't find it!" Dad shouted, anger giving the words a fearsome edge.

He came into the kitchen then. His hair was uncombed, his sleeveless white T-shirt untucked. He shot Tim an angry glance.

"Can't find what?" Mom asked.

"My gun," he replied. "It's missing. It's not in the nightstand."

Tim's mother wiped her hands on a towel and then draped it through the refrigerator handle. "I swear," she said, "if Tim took it . . . I told you to fix that lock."

The old man threw his hands up in the air, his face starting to turn red. Tim knew that look. It meant an explosion wasn't far off. He begged his mother, silently, not to push the old man's buttons, to just let it go. "Wait, wait, wait," the old man answered. "How is this my fault?"

"He's scared, Rob. Because of that story you told him. He probably took the gun because—"

Dad cut her off midsentence. "You've got to be kidding," he declared flatly. "That . . . it was just a story. A warning. My dad did the same thing to me."

"Yeah, well . . ." Mom ticked her head toward the doorway where Tim stood. "Tim has a vivid imagination."

Tim felt something, a presence, behind him, and he spun around, frightened for a second. But it was just a little boy. It took Tim a moment to realize that he was looking at himself, standing in the doorway watching his parents argue about him. Young Tim looked scared, but mostly he simply looked sad. As if this happened all the time, was a regular part of his life, and one he wished would stop.

Tim knew that was the case, remembered the feeling vividly. He had always hated the arguments. Especially when he was stuck in the middle, a weapon each used to bash the other. In this case, he recalled, his mom had been right. Dad's stories about the Boogeyman had freaked him out so much that he had borrowed his dad's gun, figuring that if anyone came out of his closet, a bullet would persuade him to go back in.

He couldn't look at his own sorrowful, young face any longer. He turned back to the kitchen, but Mom and Dad were gone, as if they'd never been there. Glancing back, he saw that young Tim was gone too. The kitchen smelled close, musty, and it looked like the rest of the house—torn up, half the floor tiles missing, cabinets partially disassembled. The old kitchen table, wood, with four chairs, was over by the window where he remembered it. A refrigerator, gray with grime, still stood in its usual spot, but there were no other appliances, just gaping spaces where they had once stood.

On the floor near the counter, though, was Lulu's red cat dish, coated with a layer of dust.

He had known coming back to this house would stir up a lot of memories—some good, but most not. He just hadn't realized how quickly they'd set in, or how vividly. He shrugged and crossed the kitchen, heading for the back hallway . . . the one the old man had come in from, in his flashback, or hallucination or whatever that had been. It occurred to him briefly that he should probably worry, probably shouldn't take that sort of thing for granted.

But if it wasn't normal for most people, it was becoming the standard for him. *Wonder what Dr. Matheson would make of that?* he thought. *Or Jessica, for that matter?*

He had had, in his youth, a serious mental problem. He'd never been diagnosed as schizophrenic, but he suspected he hadn't been far from that. If Dr. Matheson hadn't interceded when she did, he probably would have ended up there.

Now, though—he shuddered, thinking things through. If seeing things that weren't there wasn't symptomatic of schizophrenia, he didn't know what was. Dr. Matheson had made it clear that she was done with him. But she hadn't said that he didn't need a psychiatrist, only that he was too old for a child psychiatrist. She hadn't made a referral, but she'd been interrupted by that page, and then the incident with the little girl had pushed everything else from Tim's mind. If he asked, she probably would give him the referral. She was most likely still convinced that he needed one.

He wasn't sure he could disagree with her. Wasn't a sign of insanity the certainty that one was sane? If he could still question his own mental faculties, maybe that meant he hadn't gone too far over the edge yet.

When he started taking these bizarre visions for granted, that would be when he was beyond help. He determined not to let it get that far. But he wasn't going to call in the forces of medical science right now. Today, he had another agenda.

He still had to spend the night in this house. Maybe that would cure him, once and for all. He couldn't see going to a shrink before he had tried it, at least.

At any rate, it would be a lot cheaper.

Mike Halloran sat alone in his tiny kitchen, spinning a beer bottle between his palms on the yellow linoleum tabletop. He would miss Mary, he knew. She had been nothing but difficult lately, an emotional and financial drain—actually, she had been those things for more than a decade. But she was still his sister. They'd grown up together, a couple of years apart in school. He was older by nineteen months, and always felt that meant he had to take care of her.

Which, when her son had been ten years old, meant taking care of him. He had believed that she'd kick in financially when she could, but her health—mental and physical—was fragile in those days, and ever since. She had barely seemed to have enough money to make her own way, so the kid had been his charge. School, clothes, medical care, even the stint in Danville, had all come out of what Mike earned.

And Mary, naturally, hadn't had any insurance, so her stay at the nursing home and her burial expenses had been on him too. He would see a little return when he sold her house, assuming he could get it fixed up enough to sell, but in the short term, even that was a drain. He'd had to pay someone to cover his hours at the bar so he could be out there working on the place, and she hadn't made it any easier, letting it all go to hell since Rob had left.

Not that he was complaining. He wasn't the kind of guy who put much stock in bitching about the way things were. He was more the kind who simply rolled up his shirtsleeves and set to work trying to make them better. And he really did love Tim. Couldn't have asked for a better kid if it had been his own son. But he would never have one of those, of course. Was that Mary's fault too, he wondered? Had he never married because he'd shot his own emotional wad on his sister and her son?

He took another hit off the bottle, then set the

empty down on the table with its brothers. This kind of thinking did nobody any good, he figured. But what else did a man do on the day he buried the last surviving member of his immediate family? Especially a man like him, who'd made his living by pushing booze across a bar to guys trying to bury their own troubles with it. Mary's problem hadn't been booze so much as pills—*a handful a day keeps the memories at bay*.

They had all gone, first his mom, then his dad, finally his little brother, killed in a war halfway around the world. Now Mary, who had been so wrapped up in her own psychoses that Mike was never sure she knew that Jack had died, or if she remembered that she'd ever had another brother at all.

No, all he had left now was Tim. And Tim was his own man. A little scattered, maybe. Psychically scarred from everything that had happened in his childhood. Damn Rob anyway, for walking out on them like that—that had been the trigger that had sent Mary into her spiral of depression, drugs, and madness, and had done the same to little Tim.

Mike hadn't liked Rob Jensen, not from the start. Mary always said she'd met him at a nightclub, but that was a lie. She wasn't the kind of girl who hung out in nightclubs. More likely it had been a bar that was only slightly more upscale than Mike's own; maybe a little wallpaper, red velvet, like some kind of brothel. The kind of place where they pushed the champagne—the cheapest stuff they could get, but they served it in a bucket full of ice, just like downtown, and reamed the patrons on the price. That was more her speed, and definitely Jensen's.

Rob had sent her a drink from across the room, she claimed, then raised his glass to her, acknowledging her gratitude. Finally, he had come over to her, the perfect gentleman, introduced himself. They had started talking, had danced a little, and had stayed at the place until it closed, at which time he had made sure she was in a cab before he worried about how he would get home.

Mike saw it a different way in his mind's eye. Years behind the bar had given him plenty of firsthand insight into how it worked. Yes, maybe he'd sent her the drink, and waited a few minutes to approach her. But knowing Rob the way he did—and guys in general, for that matter—he figured Rob sent drinks around the joint on a regular basis, targeting girls like Mary— pretty but not sophisticated, lacking something in the self-confidence department, there with a girlfriend or two but no guys. Rob was big, muscular, swaggering, not great looking but with plenty of cocky attitude to make up for that. When he went up to Mary, he would have seemed like the height of urbane sophistication, to a naïve girl like her. Then he had sat with her, no doubt keeping the drinks coming to the table much faster than she would have done on her own. By the time the bar closed, he would have already had her phone number, maybe even stealing a few kisses and copping a feel while he helped her to the cab.

Of course, it was always possible that the cab was a convenient myth, and he'd driven her back to his place.

Either way, this conquest had stuck. Mike didn't blame Rob for that. Mary had been a doll, no two ways about that. Great figure, too. Most of the women Rob met at places like that would have paled in comparison. She'd been a beauty, impressed by him, taken in by his line—why not keep her around for awhile? Then that stretched into years, as both of them aged, gravity working its unavoidable magic on their physiques. Finally, when she and the kid both got to be too much to handle, he had taken off without warning, possibly hoping to recapture his glorious youth at some bar a couple of states away. The unbelievable way he left, the strange circumstances surrounding his disappearance, and the fact that he'd never been found didn't change that Rob had turned out to be a coward who drove both his wife and son into their own private hells.

He had seen through Rob, even back then. But Mary had been blinded by love, or lust, and had refused to see what Mike tried to point out. Next thing any of them knew, she and Rob were married, then she was pregnant. After that, Mike stopped pressing her, figuring it would be to everyone's benefit for her to stay with him and try to make things work. He had seen Rob's drinking by then, seen his nasty temper, knew the day would come when he'd start taking it out on Mary and their kid. He had tried to warn Rob to get a handle on his problem. But Rob had just blown him off, and Mary had gently suggested that he mind his own business.

So when she had that mysterious black eye one day, he had known where it came from. Not the accident with the kitchen cupboard door that she claimed. More injuries followed—bruises on her arms, legs, neck. More black eyes. Mike had offered to intercede again, but was turned away.

Finally, Tim had turned up with unexplained bruises, and Mike had been furious. Planning to have that talk with Rob anyway, over Mary's objections. It would be a talk that would be backed up with force, if need be. Mike was a tough guy—working-man tough, not bully tough, like Rob—and he knew people who knew people, if it came to that. He would not stand by while his brother-in-law abused his only nephew.

But Rob had vanished into thin air, and it seemed to put an end to that concern while opening a whole Pandora's box of new ones.

Mike went to the refrigerator, took out the last bottle of the six-pack. Unscrewed the lid. Sat down heavily, taking a big swallow as he did. It wasn't a pretty family history, but there it was. Somehow, he and Tim were the survivors.

Now they only had each other.

Ten

W hen you go back to childhood haunts, Tim thought, *things are supposed to look smaller than you remember. You've grown, you're no longer looking at them from a child's perspective.*

That didn't apply to the door, though. The door to Tim's room loomed at the end of the hallway, looking huge and forbidding. It was closed, and dark down there. The light from the ceiling fixture in the hall barely reached it, and because all the doors up here were shut, sunlight didn't leak in through the windows.

Tim approached the door slowly, cautiously, as if he might have to run away from it at any moment. His knees felt weak, like they might give way beneath him. That room—his room—was where things had gone from bad to crazy-making, where his entire young life had been turned upside down, shaken like a box of

Cracker Jack, except that the only prize that had fallen out was his dream of a happy family.

He stopped just short of the door, not willing yet to touch the knob. On the jamb were penciled notches marking his growth, with dates noted beside them. "Tim, age 4," he read. "Age 5½. Tim, 7 years old! Birthday boy!" He remembered the routine. His mom would press him up against the jamb, his back straight and head up, and lay the pencil across the top of his head while she made the little marks. She was always effusive in her congratulations, as if growing taller had been an act of will in some way, a voluntary effort on his part.

Standing out here in the hall wouldn't accomplish anything, Tim knew. He had to go in. The prospect terrified him. But Dr. Matheson had told him to face his fears. That was what he needed to do to become whole, and until he was whole he was no good to himself, to Jessica, or anyone else. "Just do it," he whispered to himself. He reached for the knob.

And as his hand closed on it, the door went away. In its place he saw strobing images of his father's supposed demise—his twisted, childhood version of it, anyway. Flesh tearing, blood spurting. He heard the splintering of bone, heard grunts of pain and screams of anguish. Through it all, he saw himself, young Tim, sitting up in bed with his eyes wide as a nightmarish scenario played out in front of him.

Tim caught himself against the wall. None of that stuff had been real. The police would have found evidence, if it had been. The physical violence Tim had believed he'd witnessed would have left marks. But it didn't. So it was all in his head.

Now, being back here, he had almost fainted, he realized, the terror of the moment had taken him away and he had blacked out for a second. He eased himself away from the door. He had to go in there, had to face his fears.

But he didn't have to do it right this minute.

Before he was halfway back to the stairs, he heard the sound of a horse whinnying outside—not a friendly nickering, but a terrified or dismayed horsey version of a scream. Opening the door to his parents' master bedroom, he passed through to the second floor porch, barely noticing missing floorboards and wallpaper half-peeled, strips of it coiled like sleeping snakes on the ground as he went. The French doors stuck for a moment but he muscled them open and went out. This porch looked out over the side of the property, toward the Houghtons' place, and he thought that was where the horse's cry had come from.

Looking down, he saw the grown-up Kate in a nearby meadow, struggling to stay mounted on top of a horse that bucked like a rodeo bronco, its eyes wild, nostrils flaring, spittle spewing from its muzzle. She fought it, but something had spooked the animal, and it seemed determined to throw her. As Tim watched, helpless from this distance, it succeeded. Kate lost her seating and flew backward off the horse. She got her feet down, tried to catch herself, then stumbled forward, landing flat on her stomach and not moving. She might have had the wind knocked out of her.

Or she might have broken her back.

"Kate!" Tim called. She didn't answer, didn't budge. Tim ran back into the house, rushed down the stairs and outside.

By the time he reached her, she was on her feet. Her clothes were stained and disheveled and she walked gingerly, with maybe a little bit of a limp, but she was upright and lucid. She looked out across the fields toward the horse, who had run far away.

"Kate!" Tim shouted, almost breathless from the unexpected sprint. "Are you all right?"

She turned slowly, maybe still a little dazed. He hoped she didn't have a concussion, but knew he needed to be alert for signs that she had. He tried to run through them in his mind, so he'd know what to watch for. Drowsiness or confusion, nausea, pupils of different sizes. Blood marked her forehead, and she wiped it off as she answered. "Yeah. I think I hit my head." She turned away again, noting the position of the horse. "I was just riding him home. He's never spooked like that before." When she looked at Tim again, she swayed, still woozy. Tim caught her arm.

"You want to come in?" he asked. "Clean that up?" Really, he wanted the chance to keep an eye on her for a few minutes before she tried to walk home.

"Sure. Thanks." She smiled as she answered him, and in that moment, Tim realized that she had grown into a truly beautiful woman. At the funeral, he had thought she was striking, but he had only seen her from a distance, and she'd been all in black, pushing a wheelchair. Hardly anyone's best look. Now she wore faded jeans and boots with a rust-colored sweater, her hair pulled back into a ponytail that had come loose when she'd fallen. Nothing glamorous about her, but her skin was fresh, her complexion starting to recover its blush after the shock of the fall. Her blue eyes were as clear and bright as her jeans, and they sparkled with intelligence.

"I saw you at the funeral today," Tim said, his mind failing to come up with anything more cogent.

"I didn't know if you remembered me," Kate replied. She offered a small frown. "I'm real sorry about your mom."

"She always liked you," he assured her. "She would've been happy to know you were there." Still holding her arm, he started to lead her toward the house. "Come on, let's go in and take a look at that."

He walked more slowly than was probably necessary, but he was still worried about shock or concussion. A few minutes later he had her sitting in the kitchen, and he'd wrapped a couple of ice cubes in a towel. "There might be some Band-Aids upstairs," he said. Emphasis on the *might*—the way the house had been torn apart, he wasn't at all sure what was where.

"This is fine," Kate replied. She took the ice, held it against the scrape on her forehead.

Tim sat down across from her at the table, and she gave him a wry smile. "I thought you were living in Boston," he said.

She shrugged, then winced a little from the effort. She would be stiff later, Tim knew. "I was. But when Dad had the stroke a couple of years ago, I figured I should be with him." She paused, caught his eye and smiled again, more broadly this time. "I mean, I was probably running away from something, but I prefer to think it's just because I'm a really good person."

Tim saw a trail of blood leaking out from beneath the ice towel. He leaned over, pressing the ice more firmly against her head. "You have to put some pressure on it."

"Ow!" she said, screwing her face up in pain. "I can manage, thank you." There was humor in her tone, though—he might have hurt her a little, but not too badly. She pulled the towel away, examining it as if there might be an important clue there. "So . . . you got a girlfriend?"

Tim wasn't sure how to answer that. It wasn't just the usual dilemma most men faced when a beautiful woman asked if they were attached—he genuinely wasn't sure. He thought he had one. But that was before Thanksgiving, before Jessica had been so pissed at him leaving the house during the night. If he had a girlfriend, wouldn't she have come to the funeral? Wouldn't she be here with him now?

But they hadn't formally broken up, so that probably meant he should say yes. "Uh . . . actually, yeah. I do." He paused for another moment before asking the appropriate follow-up. "How about you?"

Kate laughed, and he knew that his question hadn't been very well phrased—he had essentially asked her if she had a girlfriend. Which might have been the case—it had been more than a decade since he had seen her, after all, and who knew? But her answer covered all possible bases. "Nah. Just me and Dad. I'm sure some therapist would have a field day with that."

As if anxious to change the subject that she had brought up in the first place, Kate looked around the kitchen. She seemed able to ignore its present state of disrepair. "God, I remember this kitchen like it was yesterday," she said. "It's funny how your childhood stuff feels like it stays the same, even when everything else is changing."

"Yeah," Tim agreed. He was about to say more, but she went on, so he kept quiet.

"How long you staying around?"

"I think just tonight, probably," he told her. "I wanted to go through my mom's things. Pictures and stuff. I found a goofy one of you and me."

Kate shook her head adamantly, then winced again. "I don't remember ever being goofy."

"I'll show you," Tim promised. He got up from the table and went back into the living room where he'd left the photo album in the box. He grabbed the album, lifted it from the box, and was starting to carry it toward the kitchen when a loose picture slipped out of it and fluttered to the floor. He stopped, picked it up. Turned it over.

It showed his mom, standing at the kitchen sink—one of her usual haunts, and one of the places he remembered her most often when he thought about his childhood days. She looked terribly sad; her brow was wrinkled, her mouth turned down, her eyes soft and puffy, mascara streaked. Who would have taken a picture at such a sorrowful moment? Tim wondered.

Staring at the picture, he heard a voice—not his internal nag, but his mother's, as surely as if she were standing right beside him. "Nobody took your father, Timmy. He left us—and he's not coming back."

As she spoke—or as he heard it, since clearly she wasn't really there, not really speaking again that sentence she had said with such determined certainty all those years ago—the light in the closet down the hall flashed on, then off again, accompanied by a staticky electrical buzz, then another sound, a fluttering noise, as if a dozen more crows had found themselves trapped in the house. He looked, though, and there was nothing. The sounds were gone, the light was off.

"Did you find it?"

"What?" Tim asked, startled. Kate stood in the entry to the dining room, looking at him. Her head was no longer bleeding, just scraped and raw. There would be a bruise, later, maybe even a little scar. But she would be fine.

"The goofy photo," she reminded him.

"Oh," he said stupidly. He'd forgotten all about it, but he still held the album in his hands, with the picture of his mother on top of it. He flipped the album open, stuffed that picture between a couple of random pages, and then located the one of him and Katie as snowsuited toddlers. "Here," he said, handing it over.

"Aw, look at us! Even *you're* adorable."

"Thanks."

"Wow," Kate said, her voice a little dreamy. "This takes me back." She looked at him, her expression serious now. "It crushed me when you left. I came over, and you were gone. No good-bye. Nothing. Broke my little heart."

How do you think I felt? Tim thought. *My father had disappeared; my mother was having a breakdown. And I wasn't doing so well myself.* He didn't want to say that, though, didn't want to draw her attention to his own mental stability. Or lack thereof. "It broke my heart that you couldn't throw a baseball."

"And," Kate said, pointing a finger at him, as if she had just now remembered, "you were scared of closets."

Tim froze in place. He didn't remember ever telling her anything about that. Behind him, the closet light flashed again, but it only registered to him as a momentary change in the shadows they cast. Kate didn't notice anything, and she'd have been looking right at it, so he put it down to that overactive imagination his mom had mentioned. "I told you that?"

Kate nodded grimly, with fake sincerity. "I told you closets were nothing. It's the thing under the bed you had to worry about."

Tim was completely at a loss. He stood there, looking at Kate, feeling stupid. What else might have transpired between them that he'd forgotten about? He had thought his memories of his childhood were pretty clear—were there other gaps, other significant moments he had lost over the years? There had been a time when he had worried that the drug therapy he'd undergone at the institute might have caused some memory loss, but Dr. Matheson had assured him that that was very unlikely.

Kate handed him back the photo of them. "I have to

get home and start Dad's dinner," she said, heading toward the door.

Tim didn't really want her to leave yet, suddenly didn't want to be alone here in the house after all. But he couldn't think of a good way to ask her to stay. "Tell your father I said hi."

"Sure," she said. When she reached the door she stopped, looking back over her shoulder. "I bet you don't have any food in the house. Let me bring you something later."

"You don't have to do that, Kate," he answered, even though the idea thrilled him. He had to stay here, had to force himself to, no matter what. But having some company wouldn't be a bad thing. And she seemed kind of anxious to come back, too. Anyway, she was right—there was a definite consumable shortage here.

"I know," she agreed. "But it's frightening how domestic I've become."

She tossed him a final smile and left, shutting the door behind herself. As soon as she was gone, the light in the hall closet fritzed again—on, then off. This time, Tim was watching, saw the whole thing. Unmistakable. He moved toward the closet and the bulb flashed again.

Tim's blood turned to ice. Just a short in the wiring, he told himself. Uncle Mike's probably been messing with that too.

Then why are you so scared of it, Timmy? Why not just go into the closet and check it out? Give the bulb a little twist and see if you can't fix it.

He would, then. If the only way to quiet that voice was to confront his fears, he would just have to do that.

He tugged on the closet door, which swung open with a loud creak. Inside, the light socket dangled from the ceiling on a wire, with no fixture holding it in place. That probably explained it, then; a loose connection, gravity working on it all this time. All he'd have to do was what the voice had suggested, screw it more tightly into the socket. Tim stepped inside the closet, reaching for the bulb, determined to fix this little annoyance and—

The closet door slammed shut behind him, and—

The light blinked off.

It was almost pitch black inside, just some stray light leaking in around the edges of the door. Tim spun around, scrabbling for the doorknob. He felt it, smooth under his hand, hard cold metal, but then something yanked at his arm, tearing it away from the knob.

Tim looked down. In the dim light, he saw a gnarled, clawed hand on his arm, its long fingers squeezing, digging in. Tim screamed, panic overtaking him. From the darkness of the closet's depths, eyes swung toward him, beady and yellow. And more hands, bony-nailed and swollen-knuckled, nightmare hands, reaching for him, grasping, tearing his clothes, his flesh.

Clawing him. Tim flapped his arms, swatting at the hands, screaming. Fear overcame him, chased away reason. He just needed to be out. He grabbed again for the doorknob, found it, lost it, found it once again. It wouldn't turn, and more hands grabbed at him, trying to pull him back. Finally, he got a grip on the knob again, and this time it turned, the door opened, light flooded in.

Tim fell out into the hall, landing on the floor. On hands and feet, he crabwalked away from the closet, stopping only when he crashed into a wall.

With his back pressed against the wall, he forced himself back to his feet. The closet door stood wide open, light from the hall filling it. He looked in, from a couple of feet away, not yet willing to go closer. Forced himself to breathe.

Inside, clothes were tangled on the floor, and others still hung on hangers. Some of the hangers were bent and broken, seemingly by his panicked flailing.

But there was blood on his arm, seeping through his torn jacket and the white shirt underneath. Blood on his face where he had been cut—or clawed.

Something had closed the door. Something had attacked him.

Unless, of course, nothing had.

Your wounds are real, Timmy. But maybe they're self-inflicted, did you ever think of that? Did you hurt yourself? Are you too far gone, Timmy? Maybe you'll never get back. . . .

Eleven

He had been right earlier—there had been Band-Aids upstairs. Mom's bathroom was still untouched by Uncle Mike's amateur home-improvement project. Mom had been living in a care home for the past couple of years, since her health had gone downhill, and maybe they didn't want their patrons bringing their own personal pharmacies with them. In her medicine cabinet, Tim found at least a dozen expired prescription bottles, mostly for antidepressants and painkillers. Prozac, Zoloft, Xanax, Vicodin, Valium, Effexor, Ambien, Propanolol, Klonopin. Tim was amazed at the variety—it was like being in Elvis Presley's bathroom, not his own mother's.

Feeling a churning disgust at the idea of his mom ingesting all this stuff, he started to toss the bottles into the wastebasket. In there, they looked even more impressive, somehow—a mound of pill bottles, all the crap his mom had downed to get through her days. How awful must they have been, to require so much escape? How fast had she had to chase oblivion?

He closed the cabinet, and as he did, his reflection shifted, warping into something else. It was only a fraction of a second, and it could have been a trick of the light, he reasoned, something to do with the way the clouded glass moved as the cabinet door swung on its hinges.

Before he could take a closer look, though, his mom pushed past him, opening the cabinet. All the bottles he had just taken out were there again. She didn't even look at Tim, just regarded the bottles, as if it were a refrigerator and she was trying to decide what to drink. Then, apparently addressing somebody waiting outside the bathroom, she called, "I'm going to get better, Mike. I promise."

She settled on Valium, unscrewed the cap, and shook a pill into her hand. Tim watched, helpless to do anything about it. She carried the pill out of the bathroom, so Tim followed her. In her bedroom, Uncle Mike—but a younger version of him, in his late thirties, healthy and fit, his hairline just beginning to inch off his brow—watched her with sadness in his eyes. He wore a clean, short-sleeved shirt with dress pants, and had a cheap watch strapped to his wrist. Tim remembered the watch—he had accidentally ruined it, playing with it in the bathtub one night when he was about eleven. "You need to come say good-bye, Mary," Uncle Mike said.

Tim's mom put the pill on her tongue, tilted her head

back, and swallowed hard. "No . . . I don't want him to see me. Just tell him it's for a couple of months. I can't afford to sell the house, I've told him that over and over."

"But he's waiting downstairs," Uncle Mike argued.

"Mike, we've been over it," Mom said with a weary sigh. "I just don't know what else to do."

Uncle Mike shrugged. *Giving up,* Tim thought. He almost always did. His sister, Tim's mom, had been a stubborn woman, and changing her mind once she had made it up was almost impossible.

"So maybe after staying with you for awhile," Mom continued, "he'll get over it. And I'll be better too. Maybe that's what we all need . . . some time."

A sound at the door distracted her, and she looked over there, then froze. Uncle Mike stiffened too. Tim turned to see what they were looking at, though he thought he already knew.

And behind him stood young Tim—a few years older than the one he'd seen down in the kitchen before. The age, he remembered, that he had been when he finally left this house and moved in with his uncle. Not for the couple of months Mom had mentioned, but for good. Young Tim held a suitcase that was too big for him in his hands; the noise that had alerted Mom had been that, banging against his knees as he came down the hall. He looked at her for a moment, his brown eyes huge and sad, like those of a child in one of those sappy paintings. Then he turned away, still wrestling with the big suitcase, and started back toward the staircase.

Mom watched him go and sank down onto the end of her bed, burying her face in her hands. *This one,*

Tim thought, *was going to require more than one of her little pills.*

From the top of the stairs, little Tim shouted, "I hate you!" Then he descended, suitcase banging the whole way down. His words hit Mom like a shot. She jolted upright, tears springing from her eyes. Standing there watching, Tim wished he could take back the words he had so carelessly used as weapons all those years ago—words whose effect he had not seen. Maybe a different approach would have healed things, would have kept the family together. He didn't know that for sure, of course, but could only speculate based on what he knew now.

Still, there would have been more diplomatic ways to handle it.

Tim blinked, his adult self fighting back tears at the way his young life had been torn apart. When he opened his eyes again, his mother and Uncle Mike were gone, and the bedroom was back to its current state of disarray. The French doors leading out to the porch were open. He hadn't closed them since he had gone out when he heard Kate's horse, earlier. He stepped over to the doors.

Outside, the sun was sinking past the western horizon. The sky, gray and overcast all day, was underlit with pinks and deep indigoes. Soon it would be dark. Night. He had not spent a night in this house since the day he had just—what? Witnessed? Relived? Dreamed? He didn't know how to categorize what was happening. Something told him that it was meant to be this way. Maybe this was all part of the healing process Dr. Matheson had told him about. Maybe he needed to see these flashes of his former life in order to put them behind him once and for all.

He just couldn't help wishing there was an easier way to do it.

The seventh time someone stopped by her office to ask Jessica about Tim, she wanted to break a pencil between her fingers. Just to feel that satisfying snap, that pressure that indented the flesh, to smell the fresh wood and graphite scent that resulted, to hear the loud crack as it went. But the only pencils she had handy were three fat ones—twice the diameter of a normal number two school pencil—that had been a gift from an ad agency, and a couple of stainless-steel mechanical pencils. Her fingers would break before the fat ones would snap between them, she suspected, and the mechanicals were more likely to bend. Even if they did break, they wouldn't provide the same visceral pleasure.

Pencil snapping or no, she grew increasingly impatient at the queries. Then, while she bemoaned the lack of an easily breakable object, she started to think about why people were asking her. *Because they know we're in love,* she thought. *They know we are together and would be up on what was going on with each other. They probably think we've spoken on the phone half a dozen times today already.*

But they hadn't, and she thought she had been fine with that. She tried to focus on the article she was laying out, something about a homeless woman who had started a shelter for abused homeless women, and had raised money to fund it even while continuing to live on the streets herself. There was nothing in particular about it that related to her situation with Tim, but he had edited it, and with each sentence Jessica read (she shouldn't have been reading at all, she knew, but sometimes she got too involved in the stories to just ignore the content while she worked on them), she found her thoughts turning in his direction more and more.

Finally, she snatched her phone out of its cradle and punched his cell number on the keypad. Tim's phone rang and rang, but no one picked up. After a short while, an electronic voice told her that no one was available, which she had been perfectly capable of figuring out on her own. She dropped the receiver back onto the cradle. *The smarter computers get,* she thought, *the dumber they think we are.*

Part of her wanted to let this be one more thing to be pissed off about. Instead, Jessica was a little surprised to find that she was more worried than angry. She decided, on further reflection, that it had mostly been the stress of being at her parents' house—at bringing a man to her parents' house, a serious relationship kind of man, for the first time in her life—that had caused her to react as she had when he had received that call from his uncle. She should have been more sympathetic, more understanding. She was just used to being on edge around the family, to trading barbs with her dad and trying to bait him, just like when she'd been back in high school. Waiting for her sister to pull some stupid stunt. And then the way her mom had been flirting with Tim, like she was twenty instead of fifty—that had really put her over the edge.

She had been willing to let Tim ease the tension (he was good at that easing part, she thought with a slow smile), but he'd never had the chance. Crazy nightmare, and then the phone call.

But—God, it was his mother's funeral. And she had just blown it off. *Probably thinks I'm some kind of gigantic bitch now. Maybe I am.*

She had some making up to do to him. She would be doing some tension easing of her own, for that one. Lots of it. Tim was good, but she wasn't half bad herself. That was part of why they were so perfect together.

She glanced at the clock. Colson Temple liked for people to work late when deadlines were near, to stay at their desks for as long as it took to get the job done. She had fully expected to do so tonight. She'd eaten a big lunch, and brought in a frozen burrito that she could microwave later. Carbs, protein, and caffeine would keep her working late into the night.

But now she thought there was something more important she had to do, someplace she was needed more than in her office wrestling with a recalcitrant computer.

She launched her address book, scrolled through it for Tim's Uncle Mike. If anyone knew where Tim was, it would be him.

Most marriages, Mike Halloran knew, dissolved slowly, over time. With the exception of those cleaved apart suddenly through accident—a car crossing the median to hurtle headlong into a truck, a bullet through the brain at the wrong convenience store on the wrong night—whether they ended through death, divorce, or simply stagnation, there was plenty of warning.

Mike sat behind the bar he'd tended for decades and looked out at the empty room, dark and deeply shadowed, the neon beer signs turned off. A sign on the front door told potential customers that the bar was closed on account of emergency, but if that sign hadn't been there, a couple of drinkers would have been perched on stools, and at least one of them would have had his or her own tale of marital woes. Mike had never married, but he felt like he'd been divorced a hundred times, vicariously, through the stories of those who sat across the polished oak counter from him.

Even in cases where the marriage's ending seemed sudden—a husband coming home to find his wife on the living room floor doing things with a strange man that she hadn't done with him for years, a wife discovering that her husband had more interest in other men than in her—at least one of the affected parties always knew the end was approaching. And usually that party dropped clues, hints that could be read if only one knew how.

In his sister's case, there had been no warning. Maybe Rob Jensen had known—probably he had, Mike figured. His leaving must have been premeditated in some way. But Mary had been completely in the dark. Sure, they'd had their problems. Rob had a temper and a bad way of using his fists to get his way. She hadn't liked that, but she'd been willing to look past it, hoping he'd calm down sometime. There was always some extenuating circumstance, she had told Mike. Rob's job wasn't going well, debts were piling up, or his boss had yelled at him, or someone had cut him off in traffic. Aggravations that other people could just cope with enraged Rob.

Mike remembered one such occasion, right here in this bar—in the third booth from the far right corner—when Rob had lost control because someone had played "Cat Scratch Fever" one time too many on the juke box, and Mike had had to get him outside and send him home before the cops were called in. Mary had explained later that it wasn't really the song, that Rob had been turned down for a credit card that day, and he'd been stewing about it, and the song just set him off.

So their marriage wasn't a storybook one, by any means. But neither was it all horrible. They loved each other, mostly, and they had a son and loved him too.

And yet, Mike thought, *and yet . . . he up and left.* No word to anyone—not family, friends, or co-workers— no note, no letters or phone calls after he'd resettled someplace else. They had simply never heard another thing from him. He also didn't touch any joint bank accounts, didn't take any personal belongings except the clothes he'd been wearing and his wallet and keys, which had been in his pockets. His vanishing was complete, with no trace left behind.

The police had come over, of course. Normally they wouldn't even begin to investigate until a person had been missing for twenty-four hours, but when Tim told his wild, terrifying tale of his father's abduction into his bedroom closet, they had come and checked it out, just in case.

But there had been no evidence. If what Tim had claimed was true, there would have been blood all over his room, and the doorjamb would have been battered, at the very least. The cops who looked at it found nothing of the sort, though. They decided that Tim had hallucinated the whole thing, trying to explain his father's abandonment in some way that his child's mind could comprehend. That had been the beginning of young Tim's involvement with psychiatrists, and the start of his mother's slower but more complete descent into madness.

Now Mary was in the ground, finally free of the demons that had begun to torment her after her husband's disappearance and her son's psychotic insistence that his father been taken by some malevolent entity. A couple of times over the years she had told Mike that she thought Tim was right—that Rob wasn't clever enough to have vanished so completely. She had said that she regretted not taking him more seriously at the time, that forcing him into psychiatric care, making him learn to deny what his own senses had told him was true, had been a mistake. By then, however, she had been deep into her own psychoses, her periods of lucidity few and far between, and Mike had never known if she really thought that or not.

It didn't matter any more. Tim was better now, and she was gone. And if the cops or anyone else had never turned up any sign of Rob Jensen, the world was probably a better place for it.

Mike drew half a glass of beer from the tap and put it down on the bar. Then he drew another for himself. He clinked the rim of his glass against the first one, which was for his late sister. "Here's looking at you, Mary

Ellen," he said quietly. "Life was never kind to you. Let's hope things are better now." He was just about to down a swallow when the phone started ringing.

The TV didn't pick up anything out here. No cable, no satcllite. There had been a roof antenna once, but Tim didn't remember having noticed it there when he drove up. Probably part of Uncle Mike's haphazard beautification process. One of these days, Tim would have to talk to his uncle about making a plan and sticking to it.

He switched channels, again and again. Nothing came in at all. Just snow and static, and the latter reminded him disturbingly of the police walkie-talkies in the park the other night, when the cops had been looking for a missing boy.

All in all, it was probably just as entertaining and intellectually stimulating as most of what was on TV these days. Finally he clicked it off and sat in silence for a few minutes. Outside, crickets kept up their strident symphony, with bullfrogs occasionally adding bass notes. Inside, the house had been peaceful since he'd been up in his mom's room—no more visions, no more random audio hallucinations or even the usual voice inside his head. Tim had almost begun to relax. He had changed his shirt, putting on a dark T-shirt, but the house was cold inside, and he couldn't get the heater going, so he'd put his funeral jacket back on over it.

He had been avoiding the box of photos, since all looking at them did was bring back memories. That's what he was here to do, however—to face memories. So he went back to it, opened the flaps, dug into the pictures again. Color, black and white, in various sizes. He shoved pictures around, not really sure what he was looking for until he found it.

A stack of photos, rubber banded together. Tim took the stack from the box. The rubber band decomposed as soon as he tugged at it, little bits of it sticking to the top picture, which showed his dad mugging for the camera, his tongue lolling from his mouth, eyes wide as if he'd been frightened by something just behind the photographer. The picture was shot at a cocked angle, and from below, looking up. He thumbed through the rest of them. A shot of a pre-adolescent Tim taking a picture of himself in the mirror, the flash burning a white spot in the frame. A picture of Katie, fingers in the sides of her mouth, pulling her grin into a grotesque frown. An animal Tim barely recognized as Lulu, the family cat—taken from just inches away, her face was blurred out, filling the frame completely. Tim chuckled, remembering this roll—he had borrowed Mom's camera for a day and taken these shots. They had cracked him up when they'd been developed, and she had put them away for him.

The next picture didn't look familiar, though. It didn't seem to go with the rest, which had been taken in and around their home. This was a picture of a small, run-down house, with trees pressing in on it from every side as if trying to overrun it. He had no memory of the little house, or of snapping the picture. Staring at it, trying to summon it from imperfect memory banks, he frowned.

A wet thumping noise attracted his attention. He stacked the photos in his hand, shoved them into his jacket pocket, and stood. The sound had come from near the fireplace. Tim looked into it. There was a gap between the base and the remaining section of chimney, and he hadn't been able to tell which part of it the noise emanated from. As he stood there, he heard a similar sound—liquid and creepy. It seemed to be coming from the chimney section, so he stuck his head under it and tried to peer up into the darkness.

He couldn't really see anything. Not enough light filtered up from the lamps he had blazing all over the room. And it was dark up there, shadowy, which made him ill at ease to begin with. But if there was something in there, he wanted it out. He reached up, felt around for whatever it was. His hand closed on a stick, lodged inside. That was odd, but obviously it didn't belong in a chimney. He yanked it out.

When he did, something else came down—held in place by the stick, he guessed. It dropped from the chimney and bounced off Tim, landing in the fireplace. Wet and sticky and stinking to high heaven, smelling of decay and fouled soil. He gagged, brushed the crap off him that had stuck when the thing had hit him, and looked in the fireplace.

It was a cat.

Most of a cat, anyway, but the animal had partially rotted away, bits of bone and muscle visible where the fur was gone. The thing was obviously dead—but still moving, Tim realized with horror. He started to back away, feeling his gorge rise again. He still held the stick in one hand, and he thrust it out in front of him like a weapon, in case it came at him. Looking closer, he realized that the cat wasn't moving—it was crawling with maggots. Repulsed, he brushed frantically at his own clothes again, his hair, threw the stick he had pulled down to the floor. The squirming white maggots were on him, on the floor, everywhere, though most of them were contained in the fireplace.

Tim thought he would vomit. He raised an arm, held it across his mouth, and tried to look away from the sickening sight. He knew that was a bad idea, though—knew he needed to get this cleaned up fast, as disgusting as it was, before they could spread. He stomped on the maggots on the floor, then ran into the kitchen and dug under the sink until he found a plastic trash bag. Carrying it back into the living room, he opened it up and held it by the fireplace. Poking and prodding with the stick, trying to ignore the sickening squishy sounds when it jabbed through the poor animal's tattered fur and flesh, he managed to scrape the cat into the bag.

It wasn't spending another minute in this house. Even though it was dark outside and the yard was no longer as familiar as it had once been, Tim was sure he could find the trash cans and dump the bag. There had been a shed out back, and they had been stored next to that, he recalled. Turning on every light whose glow would reach into the backyard, he set out, carrying the black plastic bag at arm's length. He imagined he could feel the cat writhing inside it, but was pretty sure that was his overactive imagination again. He couldn't guess how the thing had gotten into his chimney in the first place—and more important, how it had managed to move around enough to make the thumping noise that had alerted him to its presence. But he didn't want to give that a whole lot of thought, since it seemed that it would only lead in unpleasant directions.

Outside, there was a cool breeze. The sky was dark, but a bright moon shone down, the layer of clouds that had hung on all day having finally blown over. The breeze rustled the long grass of the backyard, pushed a swing on the old rusted swing set he and Katie had played on so many times, making its chain rattle and the whole structure squeak. Shadows caused by the moonlight leaped out everywhere. Tim did his best to look past them, to focus on the lighter spots between the shadows. The big trash can was where he remembered it. He flipped the lid open, tossed the bag in, and slammed it shut again.

He sincerely hoped there was hot water in the house. He would need a long, steaming shower after his maggot bath, and after handling that wretched cat. He paused out here, though, enjoying the silvery light of the moon and this angle on his old house. He'd spent so much time out here in the backyard, playing on the swings and in the grass, that this, more than the front, was the view he remembered most fondly.

He could only stay out for so long, though. The sharp-edged shadows made him nervous, the vast patches of blackness beyond where the light reached almost terrified. He started back toward the house, then stopped, turned around.

As long as you're here, Timmy, you might as well check it out.

Tim shook his head. That voice had been gone for hours. He had hoped that by facing up to his fears, he had already succeeded in driving it away for good. *Guess not,* he thought.

Anyway, it had only said what he was already thinking. The shed. He had been deathly afraid of it as a little kid. It was dark inside, with deep shadows. Spiders lived there for sure, maybe even snakes. His dad kept gardening tools inside, and sometimes he sent Tim in to get shears, or a weed whacker, and Tim would dash in and grab whatever he'd been sent for and then leave again as quickly as possible.

After Dad had . . . after he'd left, Tim had never gone back inside. Screw the yard, he had thought. Mom hadn't made an issue of it.

Tim shrugged, steeling himself. No time like the present. He reached for the door, hesitated, then closed his hand on the latch, lifted it, and swung the door open. It was rusted and stuck when he pulled, but he tugged harder on it and it gave, opening wide with a frightful, rusty screech. Inside on the right, he remembered, was the light switch. He flicked it, thankful that, miraculously, it still worked. Two bulbs flashed on, one just over the door and the other out over the center of the shed.

The inside looked pretty much as he remembered it. Spiderwebs joined the two lawnmowers, push and gas-powered. Tools had rusted in place on their Peg-Board home. Gas cans and paint cans, a genuine fire hazard, were piled in a corner. A thick layer of dust covered all of it.

He was reaching for the switch again, to turn off the

lights, when he saw a flicker of motion behind the lawnmowers. He peered through the webbing, through the shadow. Were those eyes, looking back at him? A rat? No, too big. He kept his hand on the switch and tried to sound forceful. "Hello?"

After a moment, a little girl emerged from behind the lawnmowers. Eleven or thereabouts. She walked on stiff legs, her hands held close to her sides, and she looked up at him with terror. "Are you all right?" he asked.

She didn't answer.

"You want to come out of here?"

Still no answer. Tim backed away from the door, beckoning her to join him. She followed, out into the moonlight. "What were you doing in there?" he asked. She remained silent, and Tim kept staring at her, pieces slowly coming together in his head.

He recognized her.

"You were at my mother's funeral, weren't you?" The girl under the tree. Red sweater, striped scarf. Hair like hammered pennies. Eyes like summer sky.

She looked at the ground, at the house, at the moon. Anyplace except at Tim. Her voice was soft, almost inaudible. "My dad knew her."

She hadn't been there with any dad, though. He was sure of that. And the funeral had been miles from here. *Even,* he thought grimly, remembering his shattered, blood-streaked windshield, *as the crow flies.* "What's your name?"

She swallowed, as if he was asking her to give up state secrets. "Franny."

"So, Franny, you want to tell me why you're following me around?"

Now she was looking at him, but not at his face. Maybe his knees, or his ankles. Bolder, though. Her voice was little girlish, maybe even young for her age. Girls seemed to grow up so fast these days, he thought. This one wasn't trying to emulate Britney Spears or Christina Aguilera, though. She had an innocent quality that seemed hard to come by in this oversexed, media-hyped age. "I wanted to talk to you," she said. "I wanted to ask you something."

Now Tim was really curious. "All right."

"I got too scared."

"You want to ask me now?" he suggested.

She swallowed, moved her gaze up to somewhere around his midsection. "Is it true?"

"Is what true?"

Franny lowered her head, staring at the ground again. Tim was afraid she was losing her nerve, would never get around to her question. She bunched her hands into little fists, like she was bracing herself, willing herself to continue. "That the Boogeyman took your dad."

Who is *this kid?* Tim wondered. He stared at her, his heart suddenly hammering, a vein throbbing at his temple. For half a second he wondered if she was even real, or just another one of his crazy visions. But she looked real enough. She cast a shadow, and the details—the spot on her sweater where a little section of the lace pattern was missing, and the fraying of its cuffs, the damp spot on her knees where she had knelt in something wet—were convincing. She even smelled real: slightly earthy, like she hadn't had a bath in a couple of days.

"Look," he said at length. "I don't know where you heard that, but . . . it's just a story. There's no such thing as the Boogeyman." He realized even as he spoke the words that he was echoing phrases drummed into him by his parents, by Uncle Mike, even by Dr. Matheson. But he believed in what he was saying, so he kept on. "I was just trying to make sense of things. My dad left, and I was upset. That's all that happened, okay?"

Something changed in Franny's face as he spoke. She had finally summoned up the resolve to make eye contact, and she had been watching him with a hopeful expression. Hearing his words, her eyelids drooped, her lower lip began to tremble, even her cheeks seemed to sink in. She turned her back to him then, without saying another word, and began to walk away.

Tim felt a surge of guilt, as if he had done something wrong. He couldn't guess what, though. He had told her what she needed to hear—what he had needed when he was her age. But he didn't want to just let her walk off into the dark of night. "It's late," he called after her. "Your parents are probably worried. I'll give you a ride home. Where do you live?"

"Next to the park," Franny answered. "I'm all right. I got my own ride." She reached down into the deep grass behind the shed and hoisted up an old mini-bike, wet with dew. A cord, like on the gas-powered mower inside the shed, hung from the engine. Franny gave it a hard yank and the antique bike roared to life.

Tim couldn't let her leave without at least offering a piece of advice.

"Hey, Franny!" he called, shouting to be heard over the engine. She looked over at him as she mounted the bike. "Count to five. When you're afraid, I mean. Just close your eyes and count to five. Sometimes it works for me."

Straddling the bike, she cocked her head and narrowed her eyes at him. She looked older that way—still childish, but somehow ageless at the same time. "What happens when you get to six?" Without waiting for an answer—not that Tim had one ready—she throttled up and drove away.

Tim stood in the yard, listening until the night was quiet again. *Weird little kid,* he thought. *But she reminds me of me.*

He wasn't sure that was a good thing. He'd been one messed-up kid himself.

He went back into the shed to turn the lights out. Before he did, though, he took a last look around in there, and spotted something he hadn't seen before: a mint-green backpack with a tiny rubber frog dangling from the zipper pull and Magic Marker doodles all over its surface, laying on the ground. This couldn't have been left over from his mom—it was too clean, too new. It had to be Franny's, then. Tim picked it up, switched off the lights, and carried it into the house.

Twelve

Tim stood in the foyer at the base of the stairs, trying to decide what to do with the little girl's backpack. Open it and see if he could find an address, a way to get it back to her tonight? Maybe not the greatest idea—he didn't want to freak her parents out by having a total stranger show up at her place well after dark and toting her backpack . . . especially if she had sneaked out of the house in the first place. Perhaps wait and see if she came back for it in the morning?

Before he could come to a decision, the door to the storage closet under the stairs banged open. Tim sucked in a quick breath, startled, but then his dad and young Tim appeared and he knew it was just another memory, or hallucination. He still wasn't comfortable with these, but they were starting to become old hat.

"Tim," Dad growled, his voice tight with anger. "Look! There's nothing in there."

Young Tim sounded almost hysterical with fear. He sniffled and replied, "No! I don't want to!"

Dad grabbed him by his scrawny arm and dragged him toward the closet, yanking the door open with his free hand. Tim couldn't see if there was anything inside it from here, all he could make out was a pitch-black space. "Please, Daddy, don't!" little Tim shrieked. Tim remembered the sensation even today, the panicked, helpless feeling as the older man muscled him under the stairs.

Then Dad closed the door. Inside, in the dark, Tim lost all control. He cried, screamed, pounded on the door. "Dad! Dad! Please, let me out! Please!"

"Tim, stop it!" Dad answered. To grown Tim, the old man sounded heartless. He figured his father had just been trying to teach him a lesson—the same one he had tried to impart to Franny, just a few minutes ago. There is no Boogeyman, nothing waiting to grab you in the dark. "There's nothing in there," Dad went on. "Just count to five like I told you. Close your eyes and count to five."

Inside the closet, Tim could hear his child counterpart trying to count through blubbering sobs. "One . . . two . . . three . . ." As he reached three, the closet door started to creak open of its own accord. A strip of light from the hallway slipped inside.

Grown Tim walked over and looked in the closet. Nothing. Dust, cobwebs, a stray gum wrapper on the floor. The vision had passed.

Tim looked at his hand, almost surprised that he still held the backpack. *Having a hard time telling what's real from what ain't, Timmy?* the voice asked him. *Or is it all real? Or none of it? How are you supposed to keep things straight, anyway? And how can you tell other people what's real and what isn't, when you don't know yourself? You think you did Franny a lot of good, back there?*

"I'll worry about that," Tim answered out loud. "You just worry about who you're going to harass after I get rid of you."

No response. He carried the backpack into the living room and sat down on the couch. Turning it over in his hands, he noticed that a slip of paper had jammed in the zipper, preventing it from closing all the way. He worked the zipper, tore off a little of the paper's edge, and then got it to unzip.

Tim tried to tell himself it was her property, and he shouldn't mess with it. But it was open now, and he realized it was stuffed to the brim with sheets of paper. No wonder one had tried to get away. He tugged out the sheet that had been stuck and looked at it.

It was a missing-persons flyer. Caryl Richman, fourteen years old, last seen on April ninth. A picture showed a sullen-looking girl with bleached blond hair and dark roots, wearing a fake leather jacket and a black, torn rock band T-shirt. On the flyer were details of when and where she had disappeared, and her vital statistics. Ninety-five pounds. Five-one. Green eyes.

On a hunch, Tim dumped out the rest of the papers from the backpack. There were dozens upon dozens of them, maybe numbering into the hundreds. Some of the flyers were yellowed with age, some cut out of milk cartons, some ripped from telephone poles or other spots where they'd been stapled or taped. Boys, girls, men, and women. Every race, age, and income level one could imagine. Tim saw one that was about an entire family that had vanished in Mississippi. Others detailed the search for kids over periods of years—using the same childhood pictures, but in some cases artist's renditions of how they might look now, years after they had disappeared.

He pored over them, astonished at Franny's collection. What could possibly drive a young girl to obsess over something so morbid?

A sound caught his attention. Footsteps, running fast, somewhere behind him. They sounded like small feet—a kid's, maybe. Had Franny come back? Tim whipped his head around and caught just the slightest glimpse of a small towheaded boy racing across the foyer. Then the footstep sound was gone, as if the boy had never been there.

That was weird, Tim thought, recognizing even as it crossed his mind that "weird," for him, in this house, held an entirely different meaning than it did for most people. This had been something different, at least—not some random memory from his own childhood. And there had been a different visual quality to it, as well. When he saw those memories unfold before him, it was as if he were really back there, in that time, with whatever lighting conditions had existed then. This running child, however, had been a fast-moving blur, but clearly in the present, the light and shadow of the foyer playing off him as it would naturally.

Just nerves, he decided. Probably a sound outside, and he had only thought it was in here. And seeing things wasn't exactly out of the norm. He went back to the backpack, pawing through more of the papers that had been inside it.

They were not just missing-persons flyers, as it turned out, but a veritable encyclopedia of the missing-persons phenomenon. Franny had amassed newspaper clippings about disappearances from all around the country. "Missing Girl!" one headline screamed. "Amber Alert for Tri-County Tyke." "Family Holds Out Hope in Search for Son." There were even pages printed from online news sources, including several, he noticed, from a site called www.fear_made_real.net. Tim had never heard of the site, but then as far as he was concerned, the Internet seemed mainly good for spreading bad jokes and spam in nearly equal proportions—though spam had, in the last couple of years or so, taken over more and more from the jokes.

He read a scrap of yellowed newsprint from an Ohio paper. The article began:

> Police admit to having no leads yet in the Tuesday disappearance of seven-year-old Nicky Anders from his Cleveland home. "Nicky is out there somewhere," police spokesman Bill Krain said. "We've been turning over every stone, knocking on every door, and we'll keep it up until the boy is safe at home."

Nicky Anders had been sleeping in his room, according to his parents, when he simply vanished. Police have not been able to find any signs of forced entry to the Anders' home. The boy's bedroom is on the second floor of the house, but the window was closed and locked, as were all the doors. Mrs. Helen Anders discovered her son's disappearance when she went in to wake him for school, at about 7:30 Tuesday morning.

Early speculation centered on the parents, because of the police detectives' description of the house's condition, with all the doors and windows locked and apparently not tampered with. After extensive interrogation, though, detectives released both Ben and Helen Anders. Bill Krain, speaking for the police department, confirmed that neither parent is a suspect, and the investigation has moved in other directions.

Tim let the paper flutter to the floor. He couldn't read that anymore. He knew there wouldn't be any good news there—Nicky Anders wasn't going to be found, he was sure. He wondered if the police had checked to see if the poor kid had a closet in his room. Now *that* would have been a clue.

One of the pages printed from the Web site contained nothing but names and dates—several hundred of them. At first, he thought these must be birth dates, but then another idea chilled him to the core. Given the context, these were no doubt dates of disappearance. He spread all the pages out on the floor, covering parts of the fireplace, tools, and furniture as well. Choosing a name from the list—Vicky Sipchen, basically at random—he scanned all the missing persons notices. He didn't see her name anywhere, so he picked another one. Jayce Norbury. He repeated the process, and this time he found a flyer, with duct tape still adhered at the top. Jayce Norbury, thirty-seven, had disappeared from his home in Waterbury, Connecticut, four years earlier. This wasn't even one of those gone-to-the-store-for-smokes disappearances. According to the flyer, he had gone upstairs while the family watched TV, and had never come back down again. Reading that one raised goosebumps on Tim's flesh, remembering the dead-end investigation surrounding his own father's departure.

Tim sat down again, surrounded by the haunted faces of the missing. He realized he was shivering, as if from extreme cold. He picked up another sheet from the website, an interview with a Dr. Tomas Jaeger of Heidelberg, Germany. A photo showed that Dr. Jaeger had glasses so thick his eyeballs were almost completely obscured, flyaway gray hair that stuck up in every direction, and bad teeth. The interviewer didn't identify him or herself, but just launched into the first question.

"Dr. Jaeger, thank you for your time. What evidence has your research shown that abject terror can have a physical manifestation in addition to an emotional impact?"

Tim chuckled as he read Jaeger's response. The man

was obviously addled. *"Laboratory subjects have demonstrated a remarkable ability to physically manifest their fear in various ways,"* he said, according to this "news" report. *"I have worked, for instance, with a subject who at the moments of most extreme fear caused all the furniture in the examination room to levitate off the ground and smash against a far wall. That was a mild example, of course. Other subjects have shown much, much greater abilities, including the manipulation of time and space."*

This is nut-ball stuff, Tim thought. *I thought I was crazy, but this . . .*

He dropped the page at the sound of a muffled scream, coming from the dining room. Jumping up from the couch, he tore across Franny's collection, hurrying to the dining room door. At first, he didn't see anything, but then he looked down into the shadows beneath the big family dining table. A small hand pawed noisily at the ground. A blond boy in a blue sweatshirt stared at Tim, terror in his eyes. The boy tried to cry out, but a large hand was clamped across his mouth, muffling his screams. The hand drew the boy back, back, until he was swallowed by the shadows, and then all was quiet.

Tim bent over, moved closer for a better look. He could see under the table, see through it to the other side. There was no one down there, no place to hide. Just a pool of shadows on the hardwood floor.

He went back into the living room, pausing in the doorway for a moment. Papers were still spread everywhere. Those were real. The kids he was suddenly seeing all over the house? Not real. *You've got to keep your head screwed on,* he thought. *You can't let this stuff get to you.*

But it was getting to him, and there was no way around that. Since coming back to his mother's house, he had entered a twilight zone where the old rules no longer applied. Anything could happen here, it seemed, and the more terrifying, the better.

Maybe, he thought, *crazy old Dr. Jaeger of Heidelberg has something after all.* Could Tim be manifesting these children from his own psychic pain, his own fear at being back in this house? He had already decided that the memory/visions were some kind of manifestation caused by his presence here, so it wasn't really such a huge leap to think that he could make other things happen as well—or appear to happen, more accurately. Especially images of kids in trouble, brought on by opening nutty Franny's backpack and leafing through her collection of psychoses.

He stepped more gingerly across her papers this time, realizing that he'd torn and smudged some of them. When he sat back down on the couch, he put Dr. Jaeger aside and looked at another handful of sheets. These were photocopies from a little kids' fairy-tale book. *Hansel and Gretel. Little Red Riding Hood.* The modern versions of those ancient stories, he knew, often had happier endings than the originals. In those, people disappeared and didn't always come back. You couldn't always get Grandma out of the wolf's belly intact.

Tim scanned page after page, feeling increasingly overwhelmed by the enormity of it all. As he read he became aware of a sibilant whisper, growing louder with each passing moment. "He's gonna get us . . ." he made out, once he was able to focus on it. Then another childish voice took up a counterpoint, singing, "Don't look under the bed. That's where he's hiding . . ."

Other voices took up the chant, a chorus of them. "Don't look under the bed," they sang. "He's gonna get us, he's gonna get us." There must have been a hundred kids joining voices. Tim threw the papers down, clamped his hands over his ears. It didn't help. The singing might as well have been inside his own head— he could muffle it, but only slightly.

"I can't hear you!" he shouted at the top of his own lungs. But even that couldn't drown out the children's choir. He could no longer make out individual words—each of the children sang his of her own song, repeating a private mantra of pain and heartbreak. It all merged together into a deafening crush of noise, as if he had his ear pressed to the amplifiers at the loudest punk rock concert in history. Tim pressed his fingers against his temples. If he could have pushed through his skull into his brain, he would have. But even that might not have silenced the voices of the lost.

Their faces swam before his eyes, faces from the myriad flyers on the floor. Haunted eyes, sad mouths, grim, hopeless expressions. *Didn't anyone take smiling pictures anymore?* he wondered. *These people couldn't have all known that they would disappear, could they? Anyway, didn't I see . . . ?*

He was searching the pages for the single cheerful picture he remembered seeing, a kid in a cowboy hat with a broad smile on his face. But as he did, he realized that the scared and lonely faces he had been looking at weren't on the scattered papers at all. Instead, they were standing all around him in the room. A dozen or more. They could have been torn from these pages—several, in fact, looked horribly familiar, as he had just been looking at photographs of them.

Speechless and open-mouthed, Tim turned in a slow circle. More kids behind him, still more on the stairs. Pale, lost, frightened.

The children didn't speak, didn't move their mouths, but Tim began to hear their voices anyway. "Help us," they pleaded. "Find us, Tim. He took us . . ."

Tim thought he would surely go mad from the inescapable voices, if he hadn't already. He kept turning, hands on his head, crumpling and twisting Franny's papers with every step, turning faster and faster, spinning, really, like a top, the room a whir before his eyes—

Suddenly, the children's heads snapped toward the front door. Tim stopped his dizzying spin, glanced all around—every single one of the kids was looking that way, as if their gazes had been yanked there by strings, or directed by some signal Tim could not detect.

And then they were gone.

In less than the blink of an eye, Tim was alone again, the house silent, the voices not even an echo. He felt no relief, though. This wasn't better, just . . . different.

And the closet at the end of the hall, the one where he had hurt himself earlier, began to swing open. The hinges creaked ominously. The light didn't flash on and off like it had before—only darkness waited within.

In a way, that was worse. Tim's heart pounded, blood roared in his ears like Class 5 white-water rapids. His eyes widened, his mouth dropped open.

Inside the closet—and coming out—was the Boogeyman.

Thirteen

Tim ran.

    He had seen too much, experienced too much here. Time to get gone. He sprinted for the front door, wrestled with the knob, yanked it open.

And the Boogeyman, all black, wrapped in shadow, stood on the porch, right in front of the door. Clawed hands reaching in at him.

Tim uttered a strangled cry, all he could manage, and sank back, away from the open door.

The dark shape came inside, out of the shadows, passing into the light.

"Tim?"

It was Jessica.

Tim rushed to look past her, out onto the porch, and then spun around to check the closet. No Boogeyman in either place. Just Jessica, and a closet that was closed again.

Jessica looked at him, concern mixing with fear on her face. *I must look like a crazy man,* Tim thought. *Not far from the truth, probably.* "Where were you going?" she asked.

"We gotta get out of here," Tim said breathlessly.

"I called your uncle. He said you were here. I'm sorry about everything I—"

"I gotta get the hell out of here," Tim said again, more urgently this time. He suddenly knew escape was crucial. It was because he was here that all this stuff was happening, at his boyhood home. The place from which his father had been taken. "We gotta go. Please. *Now.*"

Jessica drove. Her BMW made a comfortable cocoon cutting through the night, its headlights slicing the darkness ahead of them with surgical precision. Tim had made her open the doors before he would even get in, so he could check out the front and back seats under the dome light. But he hadn't seen anything inside. Once they were under way and the lights went off, he was nervous again, drumming his fingers on his knee, tapping his foot. Shadows pooled in the back seat, on the floor around his feet. He didn't like that at all.

"What the hell is going on with you, Tim?" Jessica asked him as they pulled away from the house.

He tried to answer. Wanted to answer. But the words

wouldn't come. He didn't even know where to start. With the children? Franny's collection? Or farther back—his dad, his bedroom closet. The Boogeyman.

Fear made real.

Words were his stock in trade. He was educated, trained, skilled in their use. He could tell virtually any writer how to fix his or her prose, but right now he couldn't formulate a coherent explanation, could barely manage a simple declarative sentence. "I'll tell you later," he said, finally. Even as he said it, he suspected that it was probably a lie. He didn't know if he would ever be able to figure out a way to explain.

Jessica tried twice more, over the next thirty minutes or so, to draw Tim out. But caught up in his own thoughts, memories of the lost ones, of the Boogeyman coming out of the closet at him, he didn't respond. Finally, she ticked her head toward a motel, its neon sign glowing through the fog. "Look, it's late," she said. "Why don't we stop and get some rest? Talk about what's going on."

Tim just stared at the lights, gave a barely perceptible nod. Jessica pulled into the motel's parking lot. Tim looked at the lights on tall stanchions in the lot, the neon of the Travel Inn Motel sign, the soft glows emanating from curtained windows. Those were good things.

But there were still a lot of shadows around.

She parked the Beemer and climbed out. Suddenly afraid of being left alone in the car, Tim followed. She checked them in, the desk clerk eyeing him suspiciously when he refused to talk. Tim didn't care. The desk clerk, a thin, sallow man with long greasy hair, had haunted eyes and gaunt cheeks, and he reminded Tim of the missing children. *He lost someone once,* Tim decided. *That's why he looks so lost himself.*

The man rushed through the paperwork, took Jessica's credit card, and handed over the key to Room 3, just down the walkway from the office. Jessica had a bag in the BMW, but Tim had come empty-handed, still dressed in his increasingly sloppy funeral suit and T-shirt. Tim stayed on the walkway, near a droning, rumbling ice machine, while she crossed the damp, foggy parking lot and retrieved it from the trunk. When she got back, she unlocked the door and went in, turning on the light as she did. Tim followed, closing the door, setting the dead bolt and the chain lock. Then he went to the lamps mounted on the gold papered walls on both sides of the bed, switched those on. Lights over the sink, lights in the bathroom. When that was done, he stood in the middle of the room, looking at the closet door. Jessica nodded—humoring him, he was sure, even though she didn't understand. But she opened the closet and pulled the string on the light fixture inside. A few empty hangers hung on a rod, a spare pillow sat on the shelf above.

Tim felt as if he might be able to finally relax. He wondered why he had ever doubted her. She hadn't made his mom's funeral, but she had come just when he really needed her, and she was willing to do whatever it took to make him comfortable. She really was a terrific lady.

"Let's take a bath," Jessica suggested, turning to him.

She had hung her winter coat up in the closet, leaving her in a clingy white tank top and faded jeans. She came close, pressed her lips against his cheek, her breath hot on his neck as she murmured into his ear. "It's been a stressful few days, for both of us. A nice hot bath will work out all our kinks."

Tim nodded, still not trusting his own voice. Jessica went into the bathroom, and he heard the rush of water flowing into the tub. He sat on the end of the bed, still stiff and anxious. She came back out and climbed onto the bed behind him, her weight tugging at it. He felt her fingers on his shoulders, his neck. Rubbing, massaging, trying to break through the knot of tension there. He glanced up, saw Jessica in the mirror, and was comforted by that. He didn't want someone touching his back and neck if he couldn't see who it was.

"Tim, come on," she said, almost pleadingly. "I drove two-and-a-half hours to be with you."

He didn't answer, didn't know what he could say to that.

"You're going through a lot right now," she continued, ignoring his silence. "I mean, your mom just died."

And you weren't at the funeral, he thought. Saying that wouldn't help matters, he knew. Anyway, she had made up for that by coming to get him tonight. More than made up. But he felt like he had to say something, had to interact on some human level before he was lost forever, just like the missing people he had seen. Jessica was an offered lifeline, if only he could latch on to her.

"I'm seeing things," he said finally. "I'm seeing horrible things."

Jessica blew out a sigh, exasperated. That had been the wrong approach. "Tim, I can't do this. It's too much. I'm too tired."

Find us, Tim. He took us. . . .

Tim shivered but Jessica didn't seem to notice. "Can't we just forget about all the bad stuff? For one night? Just try to have some fun. Pretend that nothing else is out there."

He felt lips against his neck, checked the mirror again. Still Jessica's lips. Kissing him, her tongue darting out, touching the back of his neck. Her voice lower, now, throaty. "Listen, why don't you grab some ice. I'll get the bath ready. We'll raid the minibar and have our own little 'forget about the world' party. Okay?"

He managed a smile that he feared wasn't terribly convincing. But it seemed like Jessica wanted to believe. She returned it with one of her own, maybe a little overdone but encouraging, just the same. She kissed him once more and twisted away from him, heading into the bathroom. "I'll take a Red Bull and vodka," she said as she closed the door.

She's too good for you, Timmy. Too sweet, too giving.

She didn't even come to my mom's funeral, Tim thought. *She's here for me now but I could have used her then too.* Even as the thought flitted through his mind, he realized that arguing with himself was not a healthy sign.

You freaked her out. You scare her—and here she is

anyway. She's facing her fears head-on. Wasn't that something you wanted to do, once upon a time?

Tim had to acknowledge that it was—that had been the whole point of staying in the house. But that was before Franny and her backpack, all those missing people, and the kids running around the house, chanting at him, begging him to help them. How could he face all that?

Jessica's bath water was running, though, and she was counting on him to make her a drink. His specialty. The question of whether or not he deserved her could remain open for awhile. He was going to at least try to devote his attention to her tonight, to make her not regret having come to him. He grabbed the ice bucket off the counter, unlocked the door, and went outside.

Kate Houghton had been pleasantly surprised by the reappearance of Tim Jensen, after all this time. Meeting an old friend after a long absence was never a sure thing—more so since she and Tim had lost track of each other when they were still kids. But he had grown up something like gorgeous, and if he was still a little bit on the skittish side, he tried, at least, to present an acceptable face. He had always been a strange kid, and he remained a little off as an adult. In spite of that, he seemed kind and gentle and decent. Combine that with the gorgeous part and she was glad he'd turned up again, even if the circumstances of his visit were less than ideal.

She loved her dad, of course. With just the two of

them in the house, though, Kate had to admit she was starting to feel more than a little lonely for the company of someone her own age. Even the butcher at the grocery store in town was starting to look good to her, and he was missing a couple of his teeth, and married besides. But a girl needed to have some loving once in awhile, especially one who was used to a steady diet of it.

Boston had been a lot of things—wildly diverse, full of interesting stores, restaurants, and historic locations. It had also been chock full of interesting and eligible men. Coming from here, she had been kind of like that proverbial kid in a candy store, but with five bucks in her pocket to shop with. She had, she supposed, gone a little crazy with the plethora of choices available to her. There were weeks when it seemed like she was trying to avail herself of all of them at once.

Before too long, she had understood that some were better for her than others. Some were only available in limited ways—marriage, work, or other commitments keeping them occupied too much of the time. Some were just wrong for her. She remembered one morning waking up next to a guy with whom the only thing in common was that they were both mammals. Some were too right—she didn't want to find herself involved with her own mirror image, after all, and that one who had wanted to borrow her nail polish, "so we'll match," had been a little too similar for comfort.

And then, some were just plain crazy.

Like Max Kinmont.

Good old Max. The kind of guy because of whom restraining orders had been invented. He seemed fine at first—a little clingy, but that Kate could cope with. But then he had gone from kind of sweet to marginally annoying—showing up at her apartment unannounced, calling three or four or five times a night. Kate started to get concerned. When he confronted her while she was outside her building with another date, she broke it off with him.

That was when Max the annoyance became Max the stalker. He knew her phone numbers at work and home, as well as her cell phone. He knew her e-mail address and her street address. She found she couldn't escape him. If he wasn't calling, he was instant messaging or standing around her door. He showed up at work so often that her job was in peril.

The final straw came when she discovered she had personal e-mails that had been read—and not by her. Max was pretty tech-savvy, and he had, she was convinced, managed to hack her account. She unplugged her computer, afraid he might be rooting around in there through some backdoor entryway.

And she called the police, only to be told that there was nothing they could do unless he was proven dangerous. She had heard that story before, but always thought it was a myth. The only way someone could be proven dangerous was for them to commit a violent action, and didn't it make sense to stop that sort of thing before it happened, instead of after?

But no. That's what she was told. The best she could do, they advised, was get a temporary restraining order.

That would keep Max from coming near her, keep him from calling and harassing her.

Obviously, they didn't know Max. The TRO just infuriated him all the more. He turned threatening. Kate didn't quite get how "I love you, I have to have you" could have turned so quickly into "So, you think you're something special? I'll show you just how special you are."

Then again, she had long since stopped believing Max was sane. Around this time she had decided he probably was truly dangerous after all.

She had wanted to stick it out, to make life in the big city work for her. But her dad's stroke—she hated to think of it as convenient, but sometimes that word came to mind—had happened. She loved her dad more than anything, and by that time it didn't take much to convince her that she needed to move back here. She had left Boston with no forwarding address, and come home. Not even Max had been able to find her here.

She wasn't crazy enough to think she could just jump-start a relationship here, though. She didn't know Tim anymore, not really. It had been so long that all of their history together was ancient. He might as well have been a complete stranger who just happened to resemble an old friend. And anyway, he had told her that he had a girlfriend.

Still, that didn't mean they couldn't be friends, did it? At the very least, good neighbors.

So, as she had promised, she had prepared a plate of dinner for Tim after feeding her father—sandwiches made from leftover turkey on crusty French bread, mashed potatoes, gravy, green salad—and had wrapped the plate in plastic wrap. Now she knocked on Tim's door, and waited.

Waited some more.

Knocked again. His car was in the drive. Lights blazed inside. Had he gone to sleep already? It had been a hard day for him, but it wasn't all that late yet.

Kate tried the door. The knob turned easily in her hand. She cracked it open a few inches. "Tim?"

He didn't answer. She went inside, pushing the door closed with her heel. "Tim? It's me, Kate." Her voice echoed hollowly back at her.

As she entered farther, her gaze landed on the living room floor—carpeted in leaflets, newspaper clippings, sheets of paper of every size and color. The common thread was immediately apparent, and a chill raised goose bumps on Kate's flesh. This time, she called out louder, anxiety lending a quaver to her voice. "Tim, where are you?"

Tim stood at the ice machine, hand on the button, watching cubes shoot into his bucket. When it was full, he released the button, and the machine churned noisily.

That was okay with him. Coming over to the machine, along the lighted walkway, the darkness of the parking lot had been disturbing. He could almost hear the shadows surging toward him, like waves on a beach lapping at the sand. He preferred the racket of the well-lit ice machine.

Another sound broke over that one, and he spun around. A family had driven up, while he had been facing the machine. A woman pulled suitcases from the back of their station wagon while a man gently unstrapped a sleeping boy, probably no older than Tim was when his dad had left, while trying not to wake him. The man lifted his precious bundle from the car and carried him to the hotel while the woman went ahead with one suitcase and the room key. The man spotted Tim watching, gave him a friendly nod. Tim returned it.

Those people stood in darkness, walked through shadow, without a care in the world. They were fine. Nothing grabbed them, nothing took them away. He had never had a family vacation like that, never visited a national park or a historic site with his parents. If he started cataloguing the things his parents had never done with him, though, he would be standing here for a long time.

"There's a name for what you have, Tim." Dr. Matheson's voice came to him almost as clearly as if she'd been standing right there next to the ice machine. "Several names, actually, because you suffer from several related conditions. Achluophobia, sciophobia, nyctophobia. When things can be named, Tim, they can be treated, dealt with. Defeated."

Tim breathed a sigh of relief. He had been suffering a relapse of his childhood problems. But they were just mental disorders, "conditions," she had said. They weren't real dangers, simply his mind playing tricks on him. And they could be beaten.

Better get this ice back inside before it melts, he thought. *There's a beautiful naked woman waiting for me in there.*

Fourteen

Kate pushed through the plastic sheeting and into the kitchen. Still no Tim here, but at least every surface wasn't covered by flyers about missing people. Maybe she had underestimated Tim's weirdness after all. Papering his house with that stuff certainly wasn't normal, not by any definition she knew. And if moving away from Boston, leaving behind a psycho boyfriend, a job that was no longer fulfilling, and a few friends—running away *from*, if one wanted to be totally accurate, more than coming *to*—to live with her sick dad wasn't some people's idea of normal either, well, it still didn't come within a country mile of this kind of strange.

She put the plate down on the kitchen table. "Hello?" she called to the empty air. The house had that vacant feel to it, the way houses did when no one was around. Kate was pretty sure Tim had taken off somewhere. He had left on foot, however, unless someone had come and driven him away.

You really should get out of here, she thought anxiously.

What if he was hurt, though? What if he heard her calling for him but couldn't answer? He hadn't said anything about leaving, and he had known she would be bringing dinner by. No, before she took off she had to look around, to make sure he really was gone. She had an uneasy feeling about it—Kate wasn't ordinarily the type to snoop around; she valued her privacy and respected that of others. But that sense of unease was overwhelmed by the greater one she felt at Tim's seeming disappearance, made worse by his choice of reading material.

She went back out into the dining room, the living room. Wading through his freakish paper sea, worry gnawing at her like a dog on a steak bone. Having covered the ground floor, she stopped at the foot of the stairs and called up. "Tim, are you up there?"

Wind rattled a window and she felt her heart skip a beat. She swallowed and fought back her natural tendency, which tried to push her bodily from the house, to persuade her that here was yet another situation best dealt with by running away. *Get a grip, girl,* she told herself. *Someone's got to keep things in perspective around here. Looks like it might as well be you.*

Tim entered the motel room confidently, with only the slightest shiver from showing his back to the darkness outside. Maybe this was all he had been needing—a human connection, a reminder of what normality was—to get through his funk. Jessica had closed the closet and bathroom doors, draped her tank top over the table lamp in the room and turned off the bulbs over the bed. But the new semidarkness, which would have been terrifying just a little while before, hardly phased him. Mood lighting. Sexy. He rattled the ice in its bucket, carried it over to the table near the minibar. From the outside, he wouldn't have expected this to be the kind of place that would even have a minibar. But he was glad it did.

He opened it up, scanned the contents and price list. Coke, beer, energy drinks, and various airplane-sized bottles of the harder stuff. Bottled water at three bucks per. Milky Way bar, a buck-fifty. Cleaning out the bar would cost more than the room did. Choosing a little bottle of Jack Daniel's and a Coke for himself, the requested Red Bull and vodka for her, he swung the door shut and carried his mixings to the table. A couple of cubes of ice in each glass—"plastic-wrapped for your protection"—then a shot of Jack, some Coke on top of that. He was an estimator, not a measurer. You got to know what a shot was without having to weigh it out, when you did it long enough. You also had a good sense of when a shot was not enough. On a whim, he poured in some more Jack. He mixed Jessica's drink to the same imprecise formula.

Taking a sip of his, he winced a little. *Whew.* "I might have made these a little strong," he called to her by way of warning. "Nice job with the redecorating in here, by the way."

She didn't reply, but he heard water sloshing in the tub. He would carry her drink in to her. That would be something Jessica would appreciate. And the shirt over the lamp reminded him of just what was waiting in there.

Except for a breeze that had picked up in the last half-hour or so testing it, tugging at doors and pushing at windows, the Jensen house remained quiet. Kate climbed the stairs, calling out for Tim occasionally. She got no response. Her concern had boiled up to the point that she felt like a single giant, exposed nerve ending, and she was growing terribly afraid of what she might find up here.

Even after all these years, the layout of the house was still familiar to her, as if she had been up here a week ago instead of more than a decade. Tim's room at the end of the hall, his parent's room on the left before that, bathroom across on the right. "Tim?"

This time, Kate thought she heard a noise in response. She froze, listening, and heard it again, an indistinct, muffled sound. It could have been a low voice or a faraway thumping bass note. She thought it came from his mom's room. She tapped at the door, then opened it. She realized that she'd left her cell phone at home, didn't know if this place even had phone service. What if she needed to call 911? She'd have to run all the way back to her dad's place.

Biting back her fear, she went into Tim's mother's room. It was dark inside, a little moonlight trickling through the French doors, but the wind hadn't yet blown away all the fog, so it was filtered and dim. She could tell that floorboards had been torn up, wallpaper peeled away, but otherwise the room seemed relatively intact. A bed and a bureau and some smaller pieces of furniture were still in place. No one was inside, though, and she couldn't find any source for the sound she had heard. On shaky legs, she waited until it came again.

After a few moments, it did.

The closet.

She started for it.

"Listen, Jess, I just wanted to thank you for coming out to see me. And for bringing me here." He paused for a second, and realized he needed to add more. "For everything."

Jessica didn't respond. Tim envisioned her half submerged, with the water over her ears, her eyes closed. Just the mounds of her breasts and her knees rising above the surface. With a drink in each hand, he pushed open the bathroom door. Steam billowed out to meet him.

But Jessica was gone.

Water rippled softly against the walls of the tub, as if she had just climbed out. Tim blinked. The glasses, forgotten in his hands, slipped away, shattering on the tiled floor at his feet. "Jessica!" he called.

The tub enclosure was empty. No place else in here big enough for her. He ran back into the room, also empty, and went through it, yanking open the door. The lighted walkway was clear and Jessica's BMW still sat in its parking space, where she had left it.

Where the hell could she have gone? "Jess!" he shouted, frantic now. "Jessica!"

He noticed lights flicking on in another room. A curtain was pulled back, a face looking out, wondering who was raising holy hell in the parking lot. But no Jessica. She didn't reply; she didn't suddenly appear. He went back into the room, glancing around. A dust ruffle hung down from the mattress, brushing the carpeted floor. He dropped to his knees and forced himself to push it aside. Nothing under there but shadow.

He had seen that kid get sucked into the shadows beneath his dining room table.

That wasn't real, he reminded himself. That kid wasn't ever in the house. Jessica, though, was here. Not five minutes ago.

Gripping the edge of the bed frame, Tim hoisted himself back to his feet. Made another quick scan of the room.

There was only one other place she could be, he realized. He had known it before, but had not wanted to face the knowledge, not wanted to admit to the certainty.

The closet.

He remembered noticing that she had closed it.

She wouldn't hide in there, wouldn't play that kind of trick on him. She would know how upsetting that would be.

Are you sure, Timmy? Maybe she wants to upset you. Maybe she wants you to face your fears. That could be what this whole trip has been about—setting you up for this test.

Tim shook his head like a wet dog. Jessica wasn't inside that closet, couldn't be there.

But he had to check, just the same.

As Tim neared the closet door, all of his old fears came rushing back. *He* was *in* there, inside the closet, and he had taken Jessica. Just like he'd taken the old man—Tim's dad—and all those others, all the lost ones. He was waiting to take Tim, too, if Tim was stupid enough to open that closet door and let the shadows out.

Which means, Tim realized with a start, *he's real.*

Tim had spent years working with Dr. Matheson and other shrinks, persuading himself that he had imagined what he'd seen—his dad's abduction by something from inside his boyhood closet. He had come to believe it, just as surely as he believed the sky was blue and the grass green. He had never been able to completely shake his fear of the dark, of the shadows. He almost had to chuckle. *Completely? What an understatement.*

The point was, he had worked so hard to convince himself that his fears were unwarranted, unrealistic, and it turned out that the exact opposite was true.

He had every reason to fear the man in the dark. He was as real as Tim was.

Tim's dad hadn't deserted the family. He had been taken. Where he was taken to, Tim had no idea. He hoped he never would.

Now, the shadow man had come back. He had taken someone else that Tim loved. He didn't want to go near that closet, didn't want to have anything to do with it.

The not-knowing, the believing he'd been insane, the fears that seemed irrational and groundless—they were all preferable to what he faced at this moment.

But it's Jessica, he told himself. *And she's here because of me, to help me. If she's in trouble, I have to help her. There's really no other choice.*

He rested his hand on the knob. Glanced back over his shoulder one last time, in case there was someplace else in the room he had forgotten to look. Nothing. He pulled open the closet door.

And in the darkness, in the shadows, was motion. A blurred figure, trying to escape. Tim screamed and reached in after it, stepping into the dark.

That same muffled sound came from Tim's mother's closet. Kate still couldn't tell if it was a voice, or some kind of music. "Come on, Tim," she said angrily, although she wasn't at all sure it was really him in there. Who else, though? He had been alone in the house, and his was still the only car in the drive. Some kind of sick joke? She remembered that she barely knew the guy. "This isn't funny."

She reached for the closet door, touched the handle. "Tim?"

She was about to turn it when the door burst open, knocking her aside. A dark, shadowed figure charged out of the closet. But she was already standing to the side because of the door, so instead of slamming into her, the figure glanced off her, stumbled, and hit the floor hard. Kate couldn't restrain the scream that burst from her mouth.

When he scrambled to his feet, she saw that it was Tim. The look on his face was one of abject terror. Kate figured it just about matched her own, but her fright was quickly turning to anger. "Damn it, Tim, you scared the hell out of me!"

Tim looked around, blinking. He seemed lost, utterly confused. *Which is a familiar sensation right now,* she thought. She wanted answers, wanted to know what Tim was doing hiding inside his mother's closet, frightening her that way. "How did I . . ." he began, but he let that drop. "Where's Jessica?"

As if this whole thing wasn't confusing enough. "Who's Jessica?"

"She was here," he said breathlessly, making no sense to Kate at all. "We went to a hotel—a motel. And . . ."

"Tim, what are you talking about?" Kate demanded. She was really worried now, maybe more so than if she hadn't been able to find him at all. He needed help, she was thinking, and not the kind that she could provide.

He pushed past her, out of the room. Paused at the top of the stairs, and then thundered down them. Kate followed, trying to keep up. "Tim!"

He ignored her. Hit the ground floor and looked around. *Is Jessica one of the people on those crazy flyers?* Kate wondered. *One of the missing?* "Tim, what the hell is going on here?"

Tim stopped suddenly, and she almost ran into him. He spun around and grabbed her upper arms, squeezing hard enough to hurt. "Come with me."

"Where?" she asked. But her question went unanswered. He had already released her and dashed outside, leaving the front door wide open. She closed it behind her, giving a passing thought to the dinner she'd left inside. *Never getting* that *plate back,* she mused.

Tim ran to his car, fished keys from a pocket, and opened it up. Kate was frightened—of him, of the situation—but she didn't think he should be driving alone. *He shouldn't be out without a keeper,* she mentally amended. She had come this far, though, and figured that maybe she could help keep him out of trouble. At least make sure he didn't hurt anyone. *This is stupid,* she thought, sliding in beside him and buckling her seat belt. Tim reversed out of the driveway, hit the main road, and mashed down on the accelerator. The Mustang's wheels skidded, then found purchase on the fog-slick roadway.

Kate clutched the dashboard with both hands. "Tim, you might want to take it a little slower," she suggested.

She might as well not even have been there.

Her mind raced as Tim's car cut through the night. She was nuts for even being here with him. She had known him as a child—and he'd been an odd kid, even then. Who knew what kind of man he had really become? *You spent a few minutes with him this afternoon, he patched you up after a fall, and suddenly you're getting into a car with him? Surely you're smarter than that.*

Yeah, only apparently not. Because here you are.

Tim had retreated into himself. He drove the car, he scanned the road through a smudged and shattered windshield. What he didn't do was talk, or even acknowledge her questions. They drove into a thick fog bank, and he didn't even slow down. Kate let go of the dash, but gripped her seat cushion ferociously, as if that would save her if they ran into something.

"I took this same drive," Tim mumbled. It was the first thing he'd said in half an hour. Kate didn't have the slightest idea what he meant, but saying it made him sound almost human, and she tried to take that as an encouraging sign. She needed one, just about now. She wished again that she had brought a cell phone, but why would anyone need a phone just to drop off a plate of dinner at a neighbor's house?

"Tim, what's going on?" she asked again. "Where are we going?"

Finally he answered, but his response might have been less comforting than his silence. "I don't know," he snapped. He glanced at her and his eyes were wild, a madman's eyes. Was it just the loss of his mother that had done this to him, or something deeper? "I don't know anything," he continued. "I don't know where I've been. I don't know what I've done. I just don't know."

Yeah, that's really encouraging, she thought. *Thanks, Tim.* She wondered how long she'd have to be gone before her father noticed, before he called the state police. And maybe the National Guard.

Up ahead, red light glowed through the fog. Bright neon. Tim spotted it and stomped down on the brake so hard, the Mustang fishtailed on the damp pavement. She thought they'd flip for sure, but the wheels held on. "Oh, God," Tim said, with something like anguish in his voice. "That's it. That's the motel."

He had mentioned a motel before, she remembered.

Kate allowed herself a moment's hope that here, all would be explained to her. Tim pulled the car into the lot and brought it to a shuddering halt, parked haphazardly across a couple of spots. As soon as the car had come to a stop he twisted the key, and jumped out, pocketing it. Kate followed, trying to stay right with him. He hurried to a cement walkway with lights along its ceiling, pacing by the doors as if trying to mystically divine the room he was looking for.

Finally, he stopped in front of Room 3, grabbed the knob, wrenched it. If someone was sleeping in there, Tim was going to have some explaining to do. But given Tim's general state of mind, Kate figured, she would probably have to do the talking.

At least she could claim that he'd been drinking, if it came to that. Anybody watching him for even a moment would buy that story. She wished she had smelled booze on his breath, but she hadn't—only the sour stink of sweat. Flop sweat, she'd heard it called, tinged with fear.

When the door didn't open, Tim began to pound on it. "Jessica!" he shouted.

Kate touched his shoulder, wincing at the din he raised. "Maybe we should go to the front desk," she suggested. "And ask if—"

She let the thought trail off. Tim had reached in his pocket, and now he held a key out in front of his face like it was some kind of prize. The tag on the key had a big brass number 3 on it. Moving like he was in a trance, he pushed the key into the lock, turned it.

The door opened. Tim stepped inside, Kate right behind.

A lamp burned on a table, with a swath of white fabric draped over the shade. A couple of little liquor bottles stood on a table with two drink cans and an ice bucket. Its lid was off, and when she glanced down she saw a few stray cubes floating in a pool of water. But there was no one inside. No Jessica, whoever that was.

Tim looked at the scene before him, blinking. "I was here," he said. "We were here."

That much at least made a little sense, Kate realized. He had a key, so chances were that he had been here before. And that shirt over the lampshade didn't look like a man's. It looked like something a woman would do if she was trying to set a mood, maybe take a guy's mind off his mom's funeral or something. She had tried similar stunts herself, back in Boston. Usually when it was already too late to change the trajectory of a relationship, when the downward spiral had already hit high gear and a nasty afternoon in a cheap motel was less exhilarating than it was humiliating.

Kate circled around him, shaking those thoughts from her head like dust from a mop. Light glowed from the doorway, and she wanted to make sure the place was really as vacant as it looked. There was water in the tub, but from the door, she couldn't see anyone in the water. As she entered, fearing the worst, her foot kicked a shard of glass, sending it skittering across wet tiles. Looking down, Kate saw broken glass all over the floor, puddles, discarded jeans and underwear. It looked like maybe there had been a fight, and she realized with heightened anxiety that she had come into a motel room with a virtual stranger. "What happened here, Tim?"

His answer was offhand, as if he hadn't really heard her. "What?" Then his voice sharpened as he regained focus. "I don't know. I went to get ice and . . ."

He came into the bathroom—she could sense him, standing right behind her. She tensed. If he tried anything, put a hand on her, she would scream and fight. Her trust for him had just about gone out the window.

". . . and he took her," Tim continued. "I mean—"

Kate cut him off. She was in no mood for puzzles anymore. "Who took her?"

"You won't believe me," Tim said.

Which was pretty much true.

Because on the edge of the empty tub, Kate saw two spots of blood, almost black-red. She had seen no fresh cuts or wounds on Tim, just a tear on his coat sleeve and some scratches on his face that he'd had before.

So the blood had come from somebody else.

"Tim," she said, barely able to catch her breath. "Take me home."

Fifteen

Leaving the motel's parking lot, Tim had caught a glimpse of Jessica's BMW, sitting in the shadows. That sight convinced him that he was not crazy—well, not completely crazy. He had come here with Jessica. Something had happened to her. He just didn't know what.

But he hadn't been willing to look in the closet again, just in case.

The last time he'd done that, he had fallen into the shadows and out of his mother's closet. His stomach still churned when he remembered that trip, as if he had stepped into a *Star Trek* transporter, or something, and had come out miles from where he'd started. There had been a dizzying, twisting sensation, like some kind of bizarre carnival thrill ride, and then he had tripped from the closet and bumped into Kate.

He had never much liked carnivals or thrill rides. They relied too much on darkness for their scares. He knew that for some people they provided nothing but a momentary fright, an enjoyable frisson of unease that they looked forward to and were willing to pay money to experience.

Not him. He had always been able to get scared like that for nothing, just by turning off the lights.

The only bright side he could see to all this was that his shadow-jump proved that this wasn't all in his head. He *had* been at the motel, with Jessica, then he was at the house with Katie. Witnesses. Not that the first witness was around to give testimony, but still . . .

Anyway, he argued with himself, *it doesn't really prove a thing. What if you're only imagining that Kate is beside you now? And for that matter, what's the difference, when it comes down to it?* He had always thought the all-in-your-head thing was kind of an artificial distinction. Even when he'd been a kid and had a stomachache, and his mom had accused him of just trying to stay home from school because the illness was all in his head, he hadn't understood the concept. *So what if it is?* he had thought. *Either way, I feel crappy.*

He drove back toward his mom's house, back toward Kate's. She sat silent, huddled up against her door. He could feel her tension from here. He knew he had to try to explain. Somehow.

That would have been easier if he'd had the answers himself. "Kate, I . . ."

"Where did the blood come from, Tim?"

He shook his head. How could he respond to that? He didn't have the slightest idea, didn't remember seeing it there earlier.

"Who do you think took your friend?" There was an edge of anger in Kate's voice, as if she were pissed off by her own terror. He couldn't really blame her for that.

At least he knew the answer to this one. He didn't know how to explain it to her, though—knew from experience that to try would just make him sound completely insane. So he didn't even try.

"Tim . . . if something happened to her, if you accidentally did something . . ."

"I didn't hurt Jessica!" he interrupted. He wouldn't do that, ever.

Wouldn't you, Timmy? If you had to?

He pushed the voice away, tried to visualize a hand cramming it down into a drawer and locking it in.

But Kate echoed its query. "Are you sure?"

He steered the car, kept a steady pressure on the gas. Not too much farther now. "Everybody told me I was making it up. For fifteen years . . . ever since my dad left. Telling me over and over." Kate's father's house loomed through the fog, up ahead on the right. Tim braked for the driveway, turned into it. "But they were wrong."

He stopped the car, and she cranked open the door immediately, without another word. She ran to her front door, throwing one last look his way, and then dashed inside, slamming it behind her.

Tim sat in the car, his knuckles white on the steering wheel. It was possible, of course, that he had gone completely insane. That seemed to be what Kate believed. It was even possible that Kate herself had never been in his car at all, but was just one more hallucination. Possible, he supposed, that his mother was still alive, that he was still in Jessica's parents' house on Thanksgiving night, having an incredibly freaking awful motherfucker of a turkey-induced nightmare.

Possible, sure. But not probable.

He needed help. He was sure of that much. He didn't know what had become of Jessica, and he was certain that he'd just blown any chance of a renewed friendship with Kate, who he could have used as an ally.

He sat there in the car in her father's driveway, looking at her father's quiet house. He didn't know where to turn to help Jessica, didn't know how to reach out to Kate. Could he have lost both of them in one night? The girl he had liked most during his childhood, and the one he'd loved as an adult? It was sure looking that way now.

And he felt like he was running out of options. Call the cops? They'd lock him up in a second, as soon as he started telling his story. Normally he would have called Jessica when he was in a bind, but that door was closed to him now. Uncle Mike, maybe, though he'd been through a lot already, what with losing his sister. He pawed through his pockets, but couldn't find his phone.

Tim wasn't a guy who made friends easily, though,

so he didn't have a lot more numbers in his phone book to try. Making friends was hard when you didn't like to be out after dark or to visit strange places—places that might be full of shadows and unexplored doorways. People tended to try once or twice to get him to go out and do something after work, or on the weekend, and then they gave up.

There had been a few women, too, but those relationships had tended to end even more disastrously. Dinners in romantic, candlelit restaurants were occasions for panic, not intimate conversation. Nervous about dark places, constantly checking under the beds of potential partners—these habits of Tim's seemed to impair budding romance. But try as he might, he couldn't seem to shake them. Jessica had been the first one that had really taken off, the first woman he could truly relax with.

Early in his career, Tim had edited a story about one of those wacky old codgers who never went outside, but filled his house with books and magazines and pizza boxes—all delivered, of course—letting the trash pile up until it reached the ceiling. Then, as invariably happened, something had disturbed the careful stacks and he'd been buried under a landslide of his own refuse.

Tim was neater (he threw his garbage away, at least), but otherwise, he had become, in his midtwenties, a younger version of that codger. He had cut himself off from the world, isolated himself. Now when he really needed others, there was no one to call.

Just Uncle Mike. He hated to disturb the old guy, but he was helpless here, desperate.

Kate would have a phone.

He looked toward her house. Most of the windows were dark, with only the soft glow of hallway lights showing through them.

Behind an upstairs window, Tim saw a dark, shadowed figure flitting this way and that.

Panic gripped him like a fist around his heart. *Not her too!*

He leaped from the car, ran to her front door, and banged on it with his fists. Kicked it. Leaned on the doorbell.

Finally, Kate's face, flushed with anger, peered through the window in the door, between the curtains. "Go home!" she screamed at him. "Just go home!"

"Kate, please! Open the door!"

"Get off the porch!" she demanded.

"He's in your house!" Tim called to her urgently. The stress of the evening, all the running and driving, the fear—he was wrung out. Even so, he tried to make the importance of what he was saying clear to her. "I saw him."

The door rattled in its jamb, and a glimmer of hope rose in him. She was letting him in, or coming out. Either one would work.

But when she opened the door, she had a baseball bat clutched in her fists and a grim expression on her face. "Tim, listen to me," she began.

He tried to put on a soothing look, to disguise the naked panic that he felt. "You need to get out of this house," he said calmly.

"What are you talking about?"

"It was upstairs!" Tim insisted. "I saw him."

"My *dad* is upstairs. Probably waiting for me."

How can she believe that I'd make that kind of mistake? Tim wondered. Her dad was in a wheelchair; he didn't look at all like the Boogeyman.

"Tim," Kate went on, "I think maybe you're sick. I wish I could help, but I can't. Now, if you don't go home, I'm calling the police."

He couldn't just walk away from her. Every minute she stayed in that house, she was in danger. He had turned his back on Jessica for a couple of minutes, just long enough to get some ice, and that had been all the time he had needed to snatch her.

But if he tried to grab Kate, she would hit him with the bat. *And* call the cops. Either way, she stayed inside, and he couldn't help her. He was out of ideas, out of hope. "I *saw* him," he insisted. He sounded forlorn, even to himself. "It wasn't your dad."

"I'm going inside now. Go home," Kate said, her anger seemingly replaced by deep sorrow. "You need help, Tim."

She moved back into the dark house, closing the door behind her. Through the window, Tim saw her heading up her stairs. Nothing he could do for her now. She would go up those stairs, and she'd meet . . .

. . . who? A figment of his imagination?

"I need help," he said softly, to no one in particular.

Starting back toward his car, he realized where to look for it.

He might once have turned to Dr. Matheson. She

had always been able to calm him down before, but there was no way she would accept what he knew to be the case now. He may have been completely fucking insane, but that didn't mean the Boogeyman wasn't real. Far from it, in fact. It was the Boogeyman's essential reality that had driven Tim nuts. He didn't lose his mind and imagine that he saw his dad taken—he lost his mind *because* he saw the Boogeyman snatch his dad, right in front of him.

He climbed back into the car and pulled away from Kate's house. He couldn't afford to sit here and have her call the police. Jessica needed him, and the time it would cost him to explain himself, if he even could, would doom too many innocent people. Somebody had to do something about the Boogeyman, and if no one else would step up to the plate, it looked like it would have to be Tim himself.

The thick fog had enveloped the entire world, it seemed. Streets that might have held traces of familiarity by daylight, or even under a bright moon, were strange and forbidding in the mist. At this hour, the streets were wet, slick, and silent. A few houses showed porch lights or the soft glow of someone fighting a losing battle against insomnia, but for the most part, except for the nimbus encircling streetlights, the town was dark, asleep.

Almost by instinct, Tim found the half-remembered park. A grassy stretch, a baseball backstop and bleachers that had always needed paint, even in his youth, and a little playground. A boarded-up shack had sold burgers, ice cream, and sodas during Little League games or

July Fourth celebrations. Tim drove with his window rolled partly down, because with the fog and the spider-web of cracks on the windshield, he couldn't see through it very well, and when he heard a loud, sharp squeak he braked to a halt in the middle of the lane. He peered through the mist, looking for the source of the noise. The little merry-go-round was empty, the teeter-totter abandoned, the slide collecting moisture from the fog.

But on the swings, her fists wrapped around the chains, head inclined toward the ground, was a little girl in a red sweater and a long scarf.

Franny.

He was glad he hadn't had to go door-to-door look-ing for her. Tim parked, dug in the glove compartment for a flashlight, left the car. Memories came flooding back as he crossed the playground—spinning on that merry-go-round until he was dizzy and nauseated, laughing with Katie on the swings, summer afternoons watching Little League games, sometimes from the shade underneath the bleachers, while his dad drank beer and shouted at the umpires. He had begun to think that the only memories he had were awful ones, but that wasn't true. There had been happy times, too, even some involving the old man.

They were harder to dredge up. But if they hadn't existed at all, he wouldn't have missed his dad so much in the first place.

His shoe scuffed bare earth, and Franny glanced up at him. Her expression, thoughtful, bordering on morose, didn't change. "You couldn't sleep either?" she asked.

Had he even tried? No, he remembered—things had happened too quickly once he'd found her backpack. "Nope."

"Some nights . . . when I think he's in my house . . . I have to come out here," Franny said. She spoke so quietly that Tim had to strain to hear her. "Sometimes all night, until the sun comes up. And then everything's okay again."

"What if your parents come to check in on you?" he asked.

"I won't be there." So matter-of-factly that she might as well have added, "What a dumb question."

Tim sat down on the other swing, felt the chains biting into his hips. Franny pushed off with her toes, swinging slowly, barely moving. Distant and absorbed. "I told you a lie," Tim admitted. "The story about the night my father disappeared."

Franny glanced at him sideways, her eyes mostly whites. She was terrified. "I know."

"He took my dad," Tim went on. "Tonight he took a friend of mine. He's going to keep taking people— everyone who means something to me. He's calling me out." He realized how self-aggrandizing that was—as if he alone, out of all the people on Earth, was the Boogeyman's big concern. Franny's backpack proved that wasn't the case at all. But that was how he felt. "I need your help," he admitted.

"Why?"

"Because we're the only ones who believe."

Franny stopped her swing by digging her feet into the dirt. She didn't even look at him any more. "I have to go home," she said.

Mike Halloran heard the noise, but it was a long way off, and he tried to ignore it. Damn thing was persistent, though, whatever it was. He turned over in bed, pulled a corner of the pillow up over his ear. Still, it continued, as obnoxious and persistent as a hungry cat yowling for a midnight snack.

Finally, he climbed up out of sleep long enough to recognize it. Telephone. He pawed at the nightstand, finally dropping a hand on the thing, tugged it from its cradle, and brought it to his head. *Middle of the freaking night, this better be good.* "Hello?"

At first he thought there was no one on the other end, but after a moment he realized someone was speaking, soft and fast. He hadn't been able to make out a word. "What? Whoa, whoa, slow down. Who is this?"

She spoke up a little, but still talked in a loud whisper, as if trying not to wake someone up. *Too bad she didn't show me the same courtesy,* Mike thought. *"It's Kate Houghton,"* the woman said. *"Listen, I think Tim might be in trouble. Maybe you should go over to the house and check in on him."*

"Yeah, okay," Mike said, his own words still slurry with sleep.

"Sure," Kate said. *"You're welcome."*

Mike was about to put the phone down, but he

heard Kate's voice again, and he paused, not sure if she was talking to him. "Dad?" she said. "Is that you?"

He shrugged, hung the phone up, and sat up in bed, rubbing his eyes with his fists. He should have demanded more information from Katie Houghton, but he'd been too sleepy to think straight. Anyway, it didn't matter what she knew, or how. If Tim was in trouble, he had to get over there. First he'd try the phone, see if he could reach his nephew that way. If not, he'd just have to drive on over and see what there was to be seen.

It seemed like he had spent most of his life rescuing Tim from one thing or another. Taking the kid in when he was ten and his mom couldn't handle having him around any more, getting him through the hell that was high school. Caring for him when he'd been in the Danville Institute, and when he'd come out of it, fragile as an eggshell. He couldn't count the nights he had gone into Tim's room because the boy was crying, or screaming, sitting up in bed with his lamp on and usually a flashlight in his hands. Shadows, guys in the closet, monsters under the bed. All kids went through it, he guessed, but most of them got past it. Not Tim Jensen.

One more thing he owed Rob for, if he ever saw him again. Traumatizing his own son by walking out on them like he did.

That Katie was one sharp girl—smart, pretty, and she obviously felt something for Tim or she wouldn't have been looking out for him in the middle of the night. Maybe getting together with someone like that could calm the boy down, help him get over the fears that he'd carried around with him all his days.

It was something to hope for, anyway. Mike stretched, picked up the phone again, dialed Mary's old number, which he still knew by heart even though he'd had no reason to call it for a couple of years now.

Her phone rang and rang, but no one answered. When he tried Tim's cell, he got the same result.

With a low groan, he pulled a T-shirt from a dresser drawer, then grabbed yesterday's slacks from the laundry pile. It looked like he would be going for a drive.

Sixteen

Without another word to Tim, Franny started off across the playground. Tim didn't want her to leave. He didn't know how or why, but in some inexplicable way, she had a greater understanding of the Boogeyman than anyone else Tim had encountered. The shadow man seemed to be an obsession of hers. Tim's too, for that matter, but he had always been too afraid to study him, too scared to honestly want to know if he was real. If it was possible that with all her research Franny had discovered a way to deal with him head-on, Tim had to find out.

She walked away from the playground with apparent purpose, her arms and legs scissoring stiffly. Tim ran after her. "Franny!"

She stopped without looking back. When he caught up, he bent at the waist and legs, his hands on his knees, so he would be closer to her eye level. *Not that eye contact is a big priority for her,* he knew. "I opened your pack," he said, letting it all spill out quickly. "I saw all the pictures. All the articles. I just had to ask you something."

She answered without enthusiasm, but at least she didn't sound angry at his assault on her privacy. "Okay."

There were probably better ways to approach the topic, but with Kate in danger and Jessica already gone, Tim felt that the time for subtlety was long past. "How do you beat him?"

Franny chewed on her lower lip, her eyes downcast. Fear or anger bunched her small hands into tight fists. "I'm not sure."

Tim rose, fighting back his frustration. Franny had put more effort looking into this than anyone. If she was clueless when it came to taking definitive action, then how was he supposed to figure anything out? He followed along behind her, trying to come up with another way to pry from Franny the information he figured was locked inside her. But as he walked, his gaze came to rest on a small house outside the park, partially hidden by a copse of trees and nearly obscured by the ever-thicker fog. The place looked long-abandoned, ramshackle . . . but somehow familiar.

A sudden flash of perfect clarity struck him, and Tim dug into his jacket pocket, pulling out the photos he had stashed in there. Rifling through them, he found the picture of the little house he had not recognized before. It had been taken years earlier, of course, and in the daylight. The trees were smaller then, the weeds choking the front yard not as high, but the structure was undeniably the same. Tim felt a tingle of excitement, mixed with a healthy dose of anxiety. While he had not known the house when he'd seen the picture, or even remembered taking it, now that he stood in front of it some long-buried memory was trying to emerge through his consciousness, like a drowned body floating to the surface.

"I know that house," Tim said. He walked toward it, fixated on its faded, paint-peeling walls, its sagging roof. Chain-link fence surrounded it, but it was loose and easy for Tim to tug aside. Franny slipped through the gap, Tim following. "I've been here before."

Franny didn't reply. She shoved through the thick weeds, some of which were almost as tall as she was, toward the house. Stalks she pushed away sprung back to swat Tim as he trailed behind her. Getting closer, he saw that some of the windows had been boarded over, but others still had glass in them, coated with years of grime. No light shone from within. "I used to come talk to the old man who lived here," Tim said, remembering more about the place with every step. "Everyone said he was crazy."

The door was locked, and a yellowed scrap of some ancient notice—a condemnation, most likely—was nailed to it. The nearest window had a couple of boards nailed over it, but the glass had long since been broken out. Tim grabbed the first board, ignoring the splinters from the raw, weather-beaten wood, and pulled. Nails squeaked but gave easily, the window's frame too rotted to give purchase. He tossed that board aside and removed the next one. Now black, empty space yawned before him. Hoisting himself up, shivering from the idea of going into that darkness, he climbed inside.

I should have boosted Franny in first, he thought, but even as he turned back to offer a hand, she scrambled in effortlessly. The room was dark, deeply shadowed, and smelled of mildew and decay. Tim drew the flashlight from his pocket, flicked it on, trained it around the room. Plaster from the ceiling littered the floor, the door had been removed from its hinges and leaned up against a wall, wallpaper was black with mold.

"Are you scared?" Franny asked him, her tone making it evident that she was.

Tim saw no shame in admitting the truth. It would be insane not to be afraid in this place, at night. Not that he was making any overreaching claims of sanity anyway. "Yeah."

"Where do you go . . . when he takes you?"

Tim had been hoping *she* had the answer to that one. "I don't know."

They left this room and moved out into a short hallway leading to a combination living room and dining area. Floorboards were missing, holes had been punched through walls. Bare wires dangled from the ceiling where a light fixture had once hung. *Beautiful,* Tim thought. *Place looks like Uncle Mike decorated it.* His flashlight's beam trailed over an old couch, one of its springs pushing up through the seat and a rat's nest of stuffing exposed.

The next room was the kitchen—large appliances still in place but with their doors taken off, so they stood there like empty sarcophagi, sink full of debris, a rusted-out hot plate still plugged into a wall socket that hadn't carried electricity for at least a decade.

Suddenly Tim remembered the first time he had been inside this house. The neighborhood's older kids had warned younger ones away from it, telling stories of the crazy old coot living inside who quite probably ate small children. But almost every day Tim saw the old man who lived here. He looked older than Tim could imagine, just an ambulatory mass of wrinkled flesh in baggy orange pants and a threadbare brown sweater, even in the summer. The man either worked in his garden or just walked in circles around his house, as if searching for something he couldn't quite recall. After a few months of near daily encounters, he began to smile at Tim, and even though he was old and kind of scary, his smile seemed genuine and friendly.

They began to pass a few words from time to time, and finally, exchanged entire sentences. And after a couple of months of that, on one particularly hot summer's day, the man invited Tim in for a glass of lemonade. He had brought Tim into this kitchen, sat him down at a little wooden table, and from his refrigerator—the ruined husk of which still stood there—he had pulled out a silvery pitcher that contained the best lemonade Tim had ever tasted, before or since. Through the layer of filth overlaying everything, Tim thought he could still see the avocado green surface of the refrigerator's sides; he was sure that, in that special part of memory reserved for the finest aromas and flavors, he could still taste that perfect combination of tart and sweet and cold that the old man had poured into a jelly-jar glass for him.

Beyond the kitchen, Tim and Franny moved into what looked like a bedroom or den, a small room with no windows and only the one door. The air inside was musty. When Tim trained the flashlight on the walls, the first thing he saw was a papering of newspaper clippings stuck there. The headlines brought a shiver to his spine, and reminded him of Franny's collection.

"Local Girl Vanishes."

"Still No Leads in Missing Girl Case."

"$10,000 Reward Offered to Help Find Child."

"Police Question Father in Disappearance."

The newspapers were dated from 1961. If there had been photos, they had been torn away, as had ads and anything else extraneous to the news stories.

The man Tim remembered had been gaunt, with small sunken eyes and a face that seemed to animate only when he grinned. He had never brought Tim into this room, but had entertained him in the kitchen with stories of old-time ball games he had seen, prize fights he'd heard on the radio, and gossip about neighbors. He had mentioned a daughter from time to time, in passing, and Tim had had the impression that she had grown up and moved away. Tim recalled the man seeming lonely and appreciating the boy's company, sometimes telling his tales long into the afternoon, as if he just didn't want Tim to leave. There had been times that Tim had been a little creeped out by the guy, but at the same time, he had found the man oddly fascinating. And the man had never tried to eat him at all, or to hurt him in any other way.

This room cast the whole thing in a different light, however. The guy had suffered a serious tragedy. No wonder he had always seemed so sad and alone. As Tim moved the flashlight along the walls, its beam revealed another twist. The man had torn pages from a bible and stapled them up. Mixed among them were blank pages and torn sheets of newspaper on which he—or someone—had drawn tormented sketches of chairs and black rectangles, the pencil jabbing down so hard that the paper was ripped in spots.

Along with the drawings, he had written directly on the walls, scrawling words or names that Tim could make no sense of. "Phioras, Kenestir, Trigonon, Pliat . . ." The words jarred against one another in Tim's head, as if refusing to be translated.

"What are all these words?" Franny asked.

"He was trying to understand, trying to give it a name," Tim guessed. He couldn't have said how or why, but he thought he had a glimmer of recognition, the slightest peek into how the old man's mind had been working.

Scary, he thought, continuing around the room.

In the middle of the wall was a doorjamb with no door in it. A hammer and screwdriver collected dust on the floor, up against the base of the wall. On the other side of the jamb was a shallow closet, an empty rod across it. Tim, always nervous about closets, shone his light in.

Scrawled on the walls inside, in what looked like thick black Magic Marker—smudged by the same hand, as it wrote over and over again—and spilling out onto the jamb itself, he saw a single phrase that froze his blood like nothing he had seen yet:

face him face him face him face him face him face him

A thousand times, Tim estimated at a glance. More, probably. An insane man's Herculean effort.

And when it comes to insane, Tim thought, *I know what I'm talking about.*

He worried about Franny, seeing all this. Girl was out there on the edge as it was. She stuck close, her breathing shallow. When he caught a glimpse of her in the light, he saw tears streaming down her pale face, her nose running. *Brave kid,* he thought. *Terrified, but she's staying with it.* He was about to say something to her, but then the light fell onto an object behind her.

A chair, like an ordinary wooden dining chair or a teacher's desk chair. It was carefully placed, positioned so that it faced the closet from which the door had been removed. This, Tim could tell, was intentional.

Finally Franny spoke, her voice cracking with terror. "I don't want to be here."

Instead of acknowledging her, Tim kept his flashlight aimed at the chair, examining it. Nails had been driven at an angle into the legs, securing the chair to the hardwood floor.

Running the beam up the legs, he brought it to rest on something else, hanging about a third of the way up the front pair. Franny bent over and lifted them. Leather straps, attached to the chair. Restraints. She sniffed and gulped a couple of times before she could get her words out. "He sat here. Waiting . . ."

Tim nodded. She was right. He had put it together at the same instant. "He was trying to bring him out."

What this man had put himself through . . . Tim was horrified by the images racing through his mind. Strapped to the chair, terror darting through his body as he waited for the shadow man to emerge from a closet that couldn't be closed, no matter what. Battling his own instincts, forcing his eyes to remain open when all he would have wanted to do was to close them.

Facing the Boogeyman.

Tim realized that Franny had stepped away from him, crossing the room in the near blackness. He didn't want her far away from the only source of light, and he spun, aimed the flashlight beam at her. She had gone to a far corner where another set of papers had been tacked to the wall. Franny stared at the papers, immobile, as if she'd fallen into a trance. From here, Tim couldn't make out what they were, so he stepped closer.

"My father was trying to find me," Franny said, her voice distant, dreamlike. "Trying to beat it . . ."

Tim shone the light on the papers she was looking at. Missing persons flyers, like the ones he'd found in her backpack. Except these were all of the same girl. "Have You Seen This Child?" emblazoned in big letters across the top, photos beneath. A ten-year-old girl playing soccer, riding a bike, smiling over a birthday cake. A happy girl, with red hair and bright eyes.

It was Franny.

Tim felt like the room spun around him, like that

dizzy, drunken moment when you discovered that you would fall down if you didn't hang on to something, and even then your chances were fifty-fifty. Franny was *here*, with him. She couldn't have been ten in 1961. He studied the face on the pictures, looked at hers again. She had stopped crying. She bit her lower lip gently, but otherwise she looked calm, resolved.

But he had no doubt that it was her. What was one more impossibility in a lifetime full of them? He realized he hadn't heard the mocking voice in his head for awhile, and suspected maybe that this house was one place it couldn't follow.

"You need to go home," Franny declared, almost as if she'd read his thoughts. "You have to go to the place where it started. That's where you face him. My dad got too scared." Tim was holding his breath, listening to Franny as if she were an oracle, a font of wisdom. "You can't beat him if you're scared," she finished.

It was crystal clear to Tim that he had been dismissed. He used the flashlight to guide him out of the house. Franny followed him most of the way, but when he reached the window through which they'd come in and dropped down to the damp ground, she stayed inside. Tim turned back to her. "I have to help you—"

She cut him off. "You can't. You can only help yourself." He felt so sorry for her—lost for so long, as alone in her way as her father had been. He wished there were something he could do for her. "You were the only one who said my dad wasn't crazy."

"He loved you. Very much."

"I know," Franny said.

Tim knew it was time to go. The night sky was still dark, plenty of hours left before morning. It had to be at night, Tim was convinced. The Boogeyman could only be faced down in the dark. Anyway, Franny had done all she could for him. She had shown him the path he had to walk, if he could just summon the courage to do it.

He thought, with her example, he could at least try.

"Thank you," he said.

She smiled, and he started away from her. A moment later, he turned back, just to get another glimpse of her looking happy, as she had in the pictures on the flyers.

But the window was an empty, dark rectangle, as if she had never been there at all.

Seventeen

Mike pulled up to Mary's house and parked his red pickup. He had made that drive so many times over the years, the truck probably could have come here without his guidance. Tonight he'd had a weird feeling on the way over, as if the fog was pressed down like a pillow on the town, smothering everyone but him trapped inside their homes. The streets had been empty and still, with not even the usual nighttime sounds of crickets and frogs and howling dogs breaking the silence.

He approached the kitchen door, used his own key to let himself in. "Tim?" he called as he opened it. Tim didn't answer. Mike closed the door and went further inside. "Hey, Katie called!" he shouted. "Said things are gettin' a little loose here. You okay?"

There was still no verbal response, but Mike did

hear a noise—the sound of a power tool buzzing away in the living room. No wonder Tim couldn't hear him calling. "Aw, Tim," Mike complained. "I told you I got this job under control."

Last thing I need is him "helping" me, Mike thought. Tim had never shown much of an aptitude with tools more complicated than hammers and screwdrivers— and even then he was better with the vodka kind than the metal ones—so he was more than a little surprised that his nephew was working so late into the night. Did he think he was going to claim the house for his own, maybe cash in on all of Mike's hard labor? "Tim, you know I sunk a lot of my own cash into this place. And I've been takin' care of your mom all this time."

He shoved the plastic aside, ready to give Tim a piece of his mind.

Tim was surprised to see Uncle Mike's truck parked in the dirt drive in front of Mom's house. It was the middle of the night—what could he be doing here? Uncle Mike was, Tim knew from hard experience, a guy who valued his sleep, and could be cranky as hell if he didn't get it.

Under ordinary circumstances, Tim would be concerned about this unexpected visit. But tonight, of all nights . . . concern didn't begin to describe what he felt. Tim quickened his step, hurrying into the house. He pushed the front door open onto a dark, silent foyer. "Uncle Mike?" he called.

No response broke the quiet. Tim dashed through the downstairs, then up, taking the steps two at a time.

Flicking on light switches everywhere he went, chasing shadows away. "Uncle Mike? Hey Uncle Mike, where are you?"

Ultimately, the house wasn't all that huge, and there were only so many places one could hide . . . if hiding was what one had in mind. Somehow, Tim was pretty sure that was not what his uncle was up to. Panic threatened to engulf him. He didn't think he could stand to lose another loved one . . .

He couldn't just let himself fall apart, though. Uncle Mike's truck was outside, so he had come here. But he wasn't here now. That could only mean that he too had been taken. And still more innocent people would certainly be, unless Tim could do what needed to be done. He had to set aside his terror, shove his sorrow in a cage and lock it away.

He had to face it. Face *him*.

Are you sure you can? the voice asked, apparently back again now that Tim had returned to his former home. *You sure you're up to that, Timmy? You've been hiding from him for a long time . . . a very, very long time.*

"Shut up," Tim said out loud. "You don't even enter into it any more."

He waited, expecting the voice to keep arguing with him, but it didn't. Once he was confident that it wasn't going to, he got to work.

The first chore was to gather the tools he'd need. Uncle Mike had left stuff strewn all around the house, and Tim scooped up what he wanted—hammers, nails, a nail gun, a power drill, duct tape. There were closets and cabinets throughout the house, possible entry points for *him*. They all needed to be sealed. Tim started with the small closet under the stairs, the one his dad had shut him inside. He pried boards up from the floor and laid them across the closet, using the nail gun to drive nails through them, locking them in place. When he was finished, he rattled the closet door, but couldn't force it open.

Good. He wiped sweat from his brow with the back of his hand and moved down to the hall closet. Touched the raw cuts on his cheek from the hangers in there. That had only been this afternoon, after the funeral, but it seemed like years had passed. He took the hammer and pounded nails in at an angle, going through the door into the jamb.

The kitchen came next. He sealed cabinets with duct tape, driving screws through the doors when he thought the tape alone might not hold. The big double-doored cabinet under the sink was the hardest, but he splintered a chair with a hammer and used the slats from its back, sticking them in place with the nail gun.

Every door he approached filled him with trepidation. There was no telling behind which the Boogeyman might lurk, from which he would reach out to grab Tim as he had Tim's dad, Jessica, and now Uncle Mike. But the job had to be done. No one else was going to do it. If anyone else had ever connected the dots, they'd still have needed a Franny to put them on the right track. And even then—as with her dad, himself probably a victim of the Boogeyman—it wouldn't work if he lost his nerve.

So it was all up to Tim now. He finished with the downstairs and went up. He allowed himself a grim smile, imagining that the Boogeyman was trying all the sealed-off doors, feeling a building, seething frustration similar to what Tim had been going through all night.

Upstairs, Tim started in his mom's room. He grabbed the lower edge of her bed and hoisted it up, flipping it over, mattresses down. There would be no getting in that way. The wooden bed frame he kicked apart, using his hammer on the more stubborn sections. This gave him large wooden slats, which he nailed up against the closet door.

Sweat ran down him in rivers and he had to stop to catch his breath. It had already been a very long night, he hadn't had much sleep lately, and he was near exhaustion. But he couldn't let up yet. Too far to go, too much to do. The Boogeyman still had to be faced.

At least the battle lines had been drawn.

The confrontation would come in Tim's old room.

Tim's mom had preserved his room during all the years of his long absence, and even Uncle Mike's various home improvement projects during Mom's hospitalization hadn't made a dent in it yet.

His twin bed was made up with a red cotton bedspread, as if someone might want to sleep in it at any time. A thin layer of dust covered it, as it did everything else in the small room. A bookshelf held a scattering of books, mostly Tim's old science fiction paperbacks, and a stack of yellowed comics. Action figures and toy rockets claimed another shelf, and the bottom one was piled high with board games: Monopoly, Stratego, Clue, a few others. Between his nightstand and the bookshelf, a stained and worn Louisville Slugger leaned against the wall. Looking at it, he remembered Kate threatening him with a bat, not all that long ago. He had thought maybe they were reconnecting after all these years, but apparently that was one more in a series of bad guesses.

On the wall over his bed were drawings Tim had made. He remembered drawing superheroes and spaceships, various action scenarios, all with the unpracticed hand but unbridled enthusiasm of youth.

But those drawings were not there now. Instead, he saw different pictures, made with the same set of limited skills and all of a single subject.

The shadow man. The Boogeyman. Dark and sinister, his body twisted and warped, as if seen through a veil of heat. Tim had no memory of drawing these, but obviously he had. He was amazed that his mother had left them up. If he'd been a parent, he would have thrown them away and made his kid an appointment at—

—well, someplace like the Danville Institute.

Tim stood in the quiet room, his tools clutched in his hands. Now that he wasn't making a racket with them, he could hear the wind outside, buffeting the walls, making shutters creak and the roof groan. He looked around at his things, the remnants of his youth. On his dresser was a lamp shaped like a rocket ship. Inside, if he opened the drawers, he would probably find clothes he had last worn a decade-and-a-half ago. In the corner next to the dresser was his desk. He'd done his homework there, he remembered, unless he needed help with it, in which case it had been the kitchen table. He had sat there to draw pictures, to read. Sometimes his dad had come in and perched on a corner of it while Tim worked, offering fatherly advice and wisdom. His brand of wisdom, anyway.

Tim realized, looking at these things, that he had suffered an interrupted childhood. It had been normal, or close to it, when he was very young, but then after his father had been taken away, he'd had to try to be the adult. His mom hadn't functioned well, then or later. She'd already started with the pills. When Uncle Mike finally gave him a new home, he treated Tim almost as just another guy he happened to take care of, not as a son. Not as a child.

Tim's childhood had ended inside this room. It was unfinished business—business that would never be finished now. He couldn't go back to that.

But that didn't mean he was helpless. Not anymore.

Shoved inside the desk's foot space was Tim's old wooden desk chair. It had always been a little large for him—had been his dad's, until the old man had traded up. But it would do for now.

He pulled it out, dragging it to the center of the room. Positioning it so it faced the closet, Tim knelt down and used the cordless drill to drive long screws through the chair legs and into the floor. When he was satisfied that the chair wasn't going anywhere, he cut sections of some belts he'd found in Mom's closet and drove shorter screws through them, attaching two to the chair's front legs and one to the left arm. He

wouldn't be able to strap in both his arms, but he figured one would be sufficient. If he started to lose his
nerve, it would take him that much longer to run
away.

He yanked on the chair, but it wouldn't budge.

Perfect.

He sat down. Put his arms on the chair's armrests.
Looked straight ahead.

Into his wide-open bedroom closet. Inside, old
clothes still hung where he'd left them, so very long
ago. A chest of drawers stood up against the right wall.
On the left, the hamper where he had tossed dirty
clothes, on those nights that he remembered not to just
leave them lying on a chair. He imagined he could still
see marks on the top jamb where his father's bones had
been shattered, right before the Boogeyman had
dragged him away. But he knew that was an illusion—
those marks had never been seen again, by family or
police investigators.

Tim had propped the door open with a couple of
books, and now he stared into its shadowy recesses.
Without taking his eyes from the closet, he bent forward and strapped his legs down. Tested them. Tight.
He sat upright again, fastened the strap around his left
arm.

Expelling a deep breath, Tim pressed his back
against the chair and waited.

He tried to keep his mind from wandering. Being
back in this house set his memory racing, but dredging
up the past—and maybe restarting the vivid hallucinations he'd been experiencing—wouldn't help him now.

He needed to keep his head clear, to be ready for whatever happened. He was positive the Boogeyman couldn't resist an engraved invitation like this.

What he didn't know for sure was what he'd do when the Boogeyman showed up.

So he waited, trying to stay alert, to keep his breathing steady and even. Last thing he wanted to do was hyperventilate, take a chance on being dizzy or disoriented when the Boogeyman finally came. He stared into the closet's depths. After a long spell, the shadows in there seemed to shift before his eyes, to merge, to coalesce into a figure of some sort. Tim tensed, expectant, his heart galloping. But nothing came out of the opening, and after he blinked, the shadows had gone back to the way they were. Could have been a trick of the faint light—a cloud passing over the moon, maybe, or the headlights of some distant car striking the window.

He began to relax again, starting to wonder if maybe the Boogeyman had called it quits for the night. Maybe he had bagged his quota.

If that was the case, then Tim was willing to keep this routine up, every night if need be. The people who meant the most to him in the world were already gone, so the only urgency was protecting strangers from the Boogeyman's clutches. If it took a night, or two, or ten, Tim would be here, in the chair.

Waiting.

Sooner or later he would come. Tim would face him.

Tim glanced out the window. Still a couple hours of

darkness left out there. He'd wait a little bit longer, just to see what might happen.

As he was resigning himself to the wait, he heard a familiar sound—a low, animal moan. He hadn't heard that since he'd been in the city, but he believed he knew what it meant. The shadow man. He still couldn't see anything in the closet, though . . . where was it coming from?

Tim twisted in the chair, strained against the straps that held him down. Not behind him. Somewhere else in the house.

Then other noises joined in. They were strange at first, but within moments he could make out what they were. Nails popping out of wood. Screws tearing themselves free. Duct tape ripping, peeling itself.

Someplace in the house—maybe *everyplace*—the Boogeyman was coming through.

Everywhere *but* here.

Tim clawed at his restraints, the fingers of his free hand suddenly clumsy on the belt buckles. In the seconds it took him to free himself, the noises magnified, intensified, the racket deafening. Tim heard the clank of nails and screws hitting the floor and rolling, heard the creaking of doors. Finally released, he lunged from the chair, dashing out into the hall. At the top of the stairs, he paused.

The door to the closet under the stairs was open. The door to the closet at the end of the hall was open. He peeked into his mother's room—her closet too. The noise continued downstairs—probably the kitchen, he guessed.

The whole house was coming undone.

Where do I go? Tim wondered. *Where do I face him if he's everywhere?*

At a loss, he went back into his own room, plopped back down in the chair. He knew the Boogeyman liked closets. Sooner or later he'd come to this one.

Instantly, the house fell silent again.

Tim peered into the closet's gloom. Nothing had changed there.

"You've got to go in."

That was not Tim's internal voice, but Franny's, speaking right in his ear. Startled, Tim lurched in the chair, his own legs getting tangled in the chair's bolted down ones. Heart hammering, he turned around.

She was gone.

If she had been there at all.

Knowing what he did about Franny—which, admittedly, wasn't much, but at the same time was all he needed to know—he was sure that she had been.

He swallowed, looked at the closet. The open door swayed a little, creaking. Inviting.

She's right, he thought. *Maybe I've known it all along. I've got to go in.*

Eighteen

itting and waiting had been one thing. Tim had been frightened, but he hadn't had to take definitive action. Now he forced his stiff, reluctant legs to carry him toward that open doorway. He wondered if he should take a weapon of some kind with him. But what? He had no idea how one might hurt the Boogeyman, if he could be hurt at all. His hands quivered with terror, his palms damp. He took short, quick breaths through his open mouth. With every step he wanted more than anything to turn around, to run away.

He knew it would mean spending the rest of his life in the light, afraid of shadows, afraid of the dark. And he knew that it would mean never forming attachments with another living soul, because they would simply become targets for the shadow man. He wondered momentarily if that wasn't a price he could pay, in return for being able to walk away from this confrontation.

In the end, he knew the trade-off was no good. He had to do this, had to carry it through to its conclusion.

Whatever that would be.

Steeling himself for anything, Tim entered his closet.

And that's all it was . . . a closet. Clothes that he couldn't come close to fitting into anymore, their bottom edges hanging much farther from the ground than his current ones did. The chest of drawers, a cheap wood laminate with a few stickers adhered to its surface. The familiar once-white wicker hamper across from it. He had been in this closet a thousand times during his childhood.

There was nothing scary about it. Tim waited a moment, expecting the mocking voice to give him crap about his fears, but it didn't come. He had, it seemed, banished that. *Thank God for small favors,* he thought. Maybe that was a fringe benefit of actually facing his fears, rather than hiding from them.

Only one other thing remained to do. Tim turned, his clothes bumping him as he did, and gripped the doorknob. Once again, his hand trembled.

It continued to tremble as he slowly pulled the door closed, shutting out the light.

Leaving him alone in perfect darkness.

Perfect silence. The utter absence of any stimulus. *This,* he thought, *must be what people experience in sensory-deprivation tanks.* He couldn't imagine doing it for pleasure. Gradually, his eyes adjusted, pupils taking in the faintest light that seeped in around the door's edges, and he was able to make out shapes, if not details.

Then, the faintest sound intruded on the silence.

From the back of the closet, behind the clothes. He wasn't sure if it was real, imagined, or maybe just some clothing he had jostled. But then he caught a fleeting glimpse of motion back there—black against black, more an impression than a look.

Something . . .

Tim reached out, shoved the hanging clothes aside with both hands, making a passageway through them.

And saw—impossibly—himself. But himself delayed by several seconds. As if in a trick mirror, he watched Tim Jensen enter the closet, look around, pull the door closed with excruciating slowness, then push the clothes aside and stare at the back of the closet.

Staring at himself. Making eye contact.

Tim's world had stopped playing by the usual rules a long time ago. This was beyond strange, however, even by current standards. He turned to the front of the closet, toward the door. He thought it looked like the door was still there, but he wasn't sure of anything any more. He was losing his bearings. Was he really facing the door, or maybe the hamper? Glanced back behind him, to see if the other Tim—slow Tim—was still there.

He wasn't. Nothing was.

Real nothing.

Absolute black. The utter absence of light, of form. Deeper than shadow, because shadow requires light to exist. This was the void.

Tim couldn't look anymore. His reality was too fragile for that, the sight of nothing at all was far too terrifying. He turned away, back toward where the door had once been.

But instead of a door, he looked into a room, through a narrow space. He was close to the floor, somehow. There was carpet right in front of him, darkness above. After a few seconds, he realized he was looking at a bed, from beneath it. Box springs, a dust ruffle hanging down.

Tim crawled forward, feeling the scratchy carpeting under his fingers. The bed scraped against his back. This was impossible, but real. He could smell the dust trapped in the carpet's fibers, feel the weight of the mattresses above him. The carpet was gold and oddly familiar.

Finally, he emerged from under the bed.

He was back inside the motel room. The one where he and Jessica had been, that he and Kate had visited. Room 3 of the Travel Inn Motel.

Jessica's tank top remained draped over the lamp, creating mood lighting for an interlude that had never happened. Little bottles of liquor stood on the table, next to cans of Coke and Red Bull. Steam billowed from underneath the bathroom door, where he could hear running water.

Steam? Running water? Tim pushed himself unsteadily to his feet. Even on this night where nothing made sense anymore, this threw him. Jessica had filled the bath hours ago—then disappeared from it. They wouldn't have rented the room out to someone else already.

Certainly not without taking her shirt from the lamp and cleaning up the drinks.

The closet door was open, he noticed, a sliver of blackness showing through. He suppressed a shudder, looked away from it.

He had to check the bathroom, where he'd last seen Jessica. He called out to her, receiving no reply. Reaching the door, he pushed it wide.

Hot water roared into the tub, releasing steam into the air. The mirrors were fogged. Jessica's underwear dangled from a towel rod. Everything as he remembered it.

But there was no broken glass on the floor, no spilled drinks.

Suppressing a shiver, he moved closer to the tub, looking down into its depths. As he watched, the water from the faucet turned darker, started running black. The color of tar, of night, of liquid shadow. Within moments, all the water in the tub had turned black, shining like obsidian.

The faucet stopped, as if it had shut itself off.

A few last drops rippled the surface.

Then, all was still. Tim stared into it. It was like looking into the back of his closet, the utter emptiness of outer space. Except in space, he believed, you could see stars.

He leaned closer, and closer still, almost as if he were

hypnotized. Black or not, this was just water; he should be able to see his reflection. Unless it had become something else. He wasn't even certain it was still liquid, for that matter. Maybe it had changed, or vanished altogether, replaced by infinite nothingness. He lowered a hand toward it—

And two hands burst through the surface, thrusting up toward him.

Tim screamed.

As he tried to back away, his left foot slipped on wet tiles and his knee slammed into the tub's wall, sending a shock of pain through his leg. A figure emerged, dripping black, its hands grasping for him. A shriek tore from its awful throat, like a wet echo of Tim's own scream.

Tim found his footing, staggered away until the bathroom wall brought him up short. Through his horror, he realized that he recognized the black, flailing figure—

—and it was Jessica, gasping for breath, clutching the air for some kind of purchase, eyes wild, mouth gaping open like a fish—

—and he went to her, threw his arm out to grab her, to pull her from the tub.

She smacked his arm away, in her panic not even recognizing him. He reached for her again but she drew back, clawing at him with her nails. Slapping him.

"Jessica, it's me!" Tim cried desperately.

Ignoring her battering fists and the black slime that coated her, he leaned toward her, started to wrap his arms around her, to pull her free.

Which was when a second figure erupted from the black surface.

The Boogeyman, warped and wet.

He didn't come out of the black water so much as he was composed of it, as if it were the very stuff of shadow, and he could manipulate it at will. One of his impossible fists lashed out and connected with Tim's jaw. Tim's head snapped back, his feet skidded out from under him.

The shadow man was *real* after all. Material. Malevolent. And *strong*.

Tim's head crashed into the wall behind him. A bright burst of light, as if from a camera's flash, blinded him for a moment. He simply sat there on the floor, stunned. Immobile.

The Boogeyman wrapped his arms around Jessica, who continued to shriek, frantic now as she tried to climb out of the tub. He reached a hand up, tangled his fingers in a fistful of hair, and pushed her down. She smacked the surface with her hands, clutched at the rim of the tub. Still, he held her under.

The black goo was running off of her now, and Tim could see that the skin of her hands was pale, turning more so by the moment. Veins blue beneath it. She had never been pale like that.

Tim tried to get to his feet. Shook his head, put his palms flat against the damp tile floor to press off from.

The Boogeyman stood up to his full height, lifting Jessica from the tub as easily as if she were a child. She had lost consciousness, drowned in the pitch. The black stuff dripped away from her and Tim could see that she was pale everywhere, not just her hands. The pallor of death, he feared.

But the Boogeyman didn't shake the blackness. It clung to him as he stepped out of the tub, like a shadow emerging from a pool of shadow.

Tim got a foot beneath himself, his back against the wall. Forced himself to his feet, still dazed.

But now the Boogeyman had both feet on the floor, Jessica dangling limply from his arms, her skin almost paper white. The Boogeyman's head turned toward the open doorway. Tim knew he had to move now.

He hurled himself at the Boogeyman.

Plowed into him, making solid contact.

The Boogeyman swatted him away with one arm, as easily as Tim might swat a fly. Tim spun, once more failing to hold his footing on the soaked floor, and landed flat against the tiles. He turned his head just in time to see the Boogeyman leave the bathroom with Jessica.

Tim got a hand on the tub's rim, pushed himself to his feet again, and gave chase.

He hit the main room just in time to see the closet door bang shut.

The Boogeyman was gone, and Jessica with him.

Tim knew he couldn't hesitate. If she wasn't dead yet, she was almost there, could not have much time left in his clutches. Tim dashed back into the bathroom. If that tub was an entry point into the Boogeyman's world, he would take it. Maybe he could head them off at the proverbial pass. The bathroom was a horrific mess, oily black spots smearing tiles and walls.

But the water was clear. Tim could see the bottom of the tub, the little rubber tracks in there to prevent skids, the drain plug.

Two drops of dark blood marred the rim of the tub. He had seen those earlier, with Kate. But not when he had been here with Jessica.

None of this was possible. All of it was real. He didn't dare look at a clock, afraid that time itself would be spinning randomly. The laws of physics—immutable, or so he had believed—had been declared null and void. He thought his mind would collapse in on itself at any moment. Faced with one impossibility on top of another, how could he continue to function?

Jessica needs me, he thought. *Kate needs me. Uncle Mike.*

Franny.

He left the bathroom, went straight to the closet in the other room. Throwing the door open, he dove in.

Nineteen

He came out in a familiar hallway. It took him a moment to place it, because he had never seen it from precisely this angle before. But when he turned around to see where he had been, he saw the linen closet at the top of the stairs in his mom's house, its shelves filled with towels and sheets, the big shelf at the bottom piled high with blankets and quilts. The duct tape he had used to seal it was nowhere to be seen. He had simply walked through the closet as if it wasn't there, as if its atoms rearranged themselves to allow his passing. It would have been impossible, if that word still had meaning.

His gut churned from the passage. Breaking the boundaries of space and time had consequences, of some kind. He ignored the discomfort. No time to let something like that slow him down.

But there was no sign of the Boogeyman, or Jessica. He didn't get it. He had followed them, only moments behind. They should be here now.

Except he remembered the spots of blood, which he hadn't seen the first time—not until he'd gone back to the motel with Kate. Then they had not been there, when he had entered from his closet. Then they were, after the fight.

And the broken glasses, the spilled drinks that had been there, and then were not.

The Boogeyman wasn't limited to moving through space. He could manipulate time, as well. And moving along his shadowy paths, Tim wasn't bound by time's restrictions either. He had edited an article once by a theoretical physicist who had tried to explain, in layman's terms, how time was more fluid and less linear than most people believed. It had made his head hurt to read it, and as soon as he was finished he couldn't remember the arguments he had just read.

Now he wished he could, because maybe it would help him negotiate through the Boogeyman's multidimensional realm. Somehow he needed to get a handle on this, so he could anticipate the Boogeyman's moves, come out ahead of him, or at least close enough behind to catch him. Jessica's life—and his own sanity—depended on it.

He hurried down the stairs, into the living room. Missing-persons flyers still littered every surface, but there were power tools on the ground—tools he had taken upstairs earlier. But that (in this time continuum, anyway) hadn't happened yet. He reached out to touch a circular saw, to make sure it was real, and as he did, the tool roared into life, its blade slicing into his finger. "Ow!" Tim shouted, drawing his hand back. Blood came to the surface and Tim instinctively lifted it to his mouth, sucking at it. The saw continued to buzz, and a power drill joined in.

As he stood there with his cut finger at his mouth, he heard a familiar voice. "Aw, Tim," his Uncle Mike groused. "I told you I got this job under control."

It sounded like it was coming from the kitchen, as if Uncle Mike had come in through the other door. Tim remembered seeing his uncle's truck earlier, but not being able to find the man in the house. He started toward the dining room, hope rising in him. *An ally!* he thought. He could use some help here, that was for sure. And Uncle Mike was steady, level-headed. Just what he needed.

In the other room, Uncle Mike continued his litany of complaint. "Tim, you know I sunk a lot of my own cash into this place. And I've been takin' care of your mom all this time."

Pushing through the sheets of plastic that separated the dining room from the kitchen, Tim saw Uncle Mike heading down the other hallway, the one that would bring him out by the stairs. He followed, picking up the pace. If something had happened, or would happen, Tim wanted to get there first, to warn Uncle Mike. He entered the hallway, passing by the closet at its end. The door was still wide open. "Uncle Mike!" he shouted. "I'm right here!"

Uncle Mike turned and looked at him, a terrified

scowl on his face, but there was no glimmer of recognition there. Tim had the feeling that Uncle Mike was looking *through* him, not at him. There was something behind him that his uncle was reacting to.

Then Uncle Mike's hand swung into view, and it held the nail gun Tim had used earlier. With fierce determination, the older man aimed it straight at Tim and fired it with a loud crack. Tim tried to dodge, but the first nail shot through his jacket, pinning his shoulder to the wall. He started to tear free, but Uncle Mike kept firing, one nail after another tacking his jacket down.

Finally, Tim saw what he was firing at. The Boogeyman burst from the closet behind him, all dark malevolence, and charged toward Uncle Mike. Tim's uncle fired one last nail, then dropped the gun and ran.

They both disappeared around the corner, into the living room. Tim struggled, ripped his jacket free from the wall, and gave chase.

By the time he reached his uncle, the man was on the floor in the dining room. The sheet plastic that had been hanging up was wrapped around his head now, as tightly as if it had been shrink-wrapped there. He looked like he'd been cocooned in a massive spiderweb. Uncle Mike's mouth gaped open, the plastic indented there, as he tried to suck in air he couldn't reach. Even as Tim watched, helpless, Uncle Mike's skin started to turn pale, like Jessica's had. Throbbing blue veins stood out against it. And still, the plastic tightened, squeezing Uncle Mike's head. Tim could hear bones popping, could see blood start to fill the plastic. Uncle Mike's hand reached out blindly, and Tim instinctively grasped it—

—and felt the older man's flesh!

Tim had thought that he wouldn't be able to touch Uncle Mike. The man hadn't seen him or heard him, so he thought they were somehow existing on different planes at the same time, or maybe different times in the same plane.

But they could touch. Uncle Mike's hand closed on his, desperation making him squeeze tightly. Tim realized he still had time, he had to do something. He tried to rip the plastic off Uncle Mike's head, but it wouldn't give. It was too snug already; Tim's fingers, damp with sweat, only slid off its surface. He scanned the room quickly, his eyes lighting on a carpet knife. He shook free of Uncle Mike's grasp and dove for it. When he returned with the knife, he could see the older man looking through the plastic, his eyes wide with terror, but seemingly finding some comfort at Tim's presence.

Before Tim could slice the plastic, though, Uncle Mike's eyes widened more, his hands flailing at empty air, his mouth working in a silent scream.

Tim risked a glance over his shoulder.

And the Boogeyman, coming from nowhere, had Uncle Mike's legs. Yanked him out from under Tim, and dragged him, head bouncing, back into the hall. Tim threw the knife aside and followed again.

In the hallway, the Boogeyman hauled Uncle Mike into the closet. Tim raced inside after them, intent on staying close behind.

Swirling darkness greeted him, and the now-familiar

dizzy wrenching of his gut. Then he saw a door in front of him. He shoved it open, fell out.

And knocked Kate to the ground as he did.

Her room, he guessed, in her dad's house.

"What the hell was that?" Kate demanded, panic making her voice shrill.

Tim lunged to his feet, went back to her closet door, yanked it open. Just a closet now, with her clothes hanging from rods, her shoes on the floor. Small boxes and photo albums piled on a shelf at the top.

"I don't understand—" Tim began.

"Understand what?"

He was about to answer when she was jerked to the floor and under the bed by her ankles, like a swimmer being pulled under the waves by a shark. She screamed and Tim threw himself to the floor, reaching for her.

He caught her right arm. Holding onto it, he felt himself being dragged forward too. The darkness under the bed yawned like an open mouth, intent on swallowing them both. He braced himself against one of the bed's legs, determined to hold her here. The floor was hard and cool beneath him, and he mentally clung to that bit of reality, like a lifeline for his sanity.

"Tim!" Kate cried, panic in her voice.

"I won't let go this time!" he swore. "I won't let go!"

Kate's appeal was frantic, heartbreaking. "Tim, help me!"

With the bed's legs biting into his feet, Tim pulled her with all his might, his shoulders and back straining with the effort. He sat as if he were rowing against an incredibly powerful current.

He felt the Boogeyman's resistance. The shadow man didn't like to lose. He was a stubborn bastard, Tim was learning.

Well, Tim could be stubborn, too.

He pulled and felt Kate slide toward him. Maybe an inch or so. Something, though. He put even more into it. Pulled.

Another inch, and then another. Slowly, Kate was coming his way. She sobbed, her eyes locked on Tim's, pleading. He pulled.

Finally, he broke the Boogeyman's grip, and Kate came into his arms. He enveloped her, rolling away from the bed. Quickly, before anything else could happen, he pushed to his feet, helped Kate up. They stood there for a moment, arms wrapped around each other as if they were the last two humans on Earth. Maybe they were. At this moment, Tim felt an enormous sense of relief, of triumph. At least he had saved one life.

But the Boogeyman erupted from the darkness under the bed again, clutching for his prize. Tim, startled, drew back, taking Kate with him. Her legs tangled with his, and they fell toward her closet door.

At the last moment, Tim knew that the closet was their salvation. If the Boogeyman could use its passageways to avoid him, he could do the same. He staggered to keep his balance without losing Kate. With every ounce of strength he could muster, he hauled her inside, slamming the door behind them.

They fell out in Tim's room, back at his mom's house. But not Tim's room as it was now, as he had left it tonight. Tim's room as it had been when he was a boy. His mom had maintained it as well as she could, but there were things he had lost or broken, long ago, that weren't in it anymore.

But they were all here now. Contained lightning flashed within his nebula ball. A strangely sinister plastic bird hung from the ceiling—he couldn't help wondering why he had ever thought that was cool. His chair—somehow, still screwed to the floor, the leather belt segments dangling from it—was piled with dirty laundry, a bathrobe draped over the back of it. He was beyond wondering how or why; he just accepted what he saw.

Kate hadn't been through everything he had, though—didn't know that this kind of thing had become par for the course. Her fingers dug into Tim's flesh. He tried to pry himself free, but she was in shock, her eyes glassy, her hands curled into claws. "Get up," Tim urged, finding his own footing. "You've got to get out of here."

She didn't answer, didn't move except for the shuddering of her body as deep-throated sobs wracked it. Tim knew how she felt. A few hours of crying wouldn't have been a bad idea, he figured, except that they were probably still being chased.

"It's okay," he said, wiping hair from her eyes with his free hand. "I won't let him take you." He didn't know if he could keep that promise, but he had to try. She nodded offhandedly, as if she hadn't quite heard him but was willing to go along anyway. Tim helped Kate to her feet, but her legs were shaking and he wasn't at all sure they would offer support if he released her.

She seemed to sense what he was thinking. "Don't," she began, but a hitch in her voice cut her off. "Don't let go of me," she managed.

Tim was about to answer, but something about the room changed. The quality of the light, maybe. He heard a distant rumble, coming closer, like a train nearing the platform from a subway tunnel. "He's coming back," Tim warned. "Go!"

He twisted himself out of Kate's grasp. She swayed unsteadily. He had to get her away before the Boogeyman came back, though. He knew he needed to face the Boogeyman, one-on-one, without having to worry about his loved ones. He could hold the shadow man while she made a break for freedom. "You have to get away from me," Tim urged.

He pushed Kate aside and turned toward the closet door.

"Come out!" he challenged. "Let me see you."

As if in response, the door swung open. Inside, shadows gathered, taking shape. Then, as if shot from a cannon, the Boogeyman burst out, coming to a halt directly in front of Tim. A powerful wind blew out around him, lifting Tim from his feet and hurling him to the floor. Kate smashed into a wall in the far corner of the room.

Tim closed his eyes as the Boogeyman loomed before him. He was on his back, helpless. He had only one weapon at his disposal, and he had a feeling it wasn't good enough.

"One."

He knew death was imminent, that knowledge made more concrete by the images flashing in his mind's eye. Himself as a small boy, huddled under his covers as thunder crashed outside his room and lightning etched stark shadows on the walls.

"Two."

A menacing action figure standing on his nightstand in the dark.

"Three."

His bathrobe draped over a chair, making a shape like a hunched nightmare creature.

"Four."

His nebula ball, crackling with its own internal lightning.

"Five."

A suspended black bird flapping its wings in a faint breeze, as if some force had brought it to life.

"Six."

What happens when you get to six? Franny had asked. He hadn't known what the answer was.

He was about to find out.

Twenty

Tim stood up, opening his eyes. His dad's old trick, the banishing spell of counting to five, hadn't worked. The Boogeyman was still there in front of him, his arms at his sides. Black as black could be. The emptiness of the void. Eyes mere indentations in the darkness of his evil face.

Tim looked into those eyes, seeing nothing there. He thought there should be menace in them, or intelligence. Something that could be reasoned or argued with. But the Boogeyman was not, he decided, sentient, at least as he understood the term. He was more elemental than that. He was hunger, horror, darkness. States of being, more than a being in his own right. Which made him even more terrifying, because he was ultimately unknowable. This guy was not some cuddly monster who could be empathized with. He couldn't even be understood. Like evil itself, he simply was.

But suddenly, Tim thought that he could be defeated. "I brought you into this world," he declared. He didn't know where his certainty had come from, but he felt it just the same. "I can take you out of it."

He backed toward his bed, toward the baseball bat he knew leaned against the wall beside it. Risking only the briefest of glances behind him, he closed a hand on the bat, lifted it from the spot it had occupied for so long. The wood, polished from hard use, felt comfortable in his grasp, familiar, as if his hands were still the same size they'd always been. He raised the bat toward his enemy.

The Boogeyman smiled at it. It was not, Tim thought, a terribly impressive weapon.

But it'll do the job, Tim suddenly knew. And at the same moment, he understood what he had to do.

What he didn't know about his opponent would always, he was certain, trump what he could know. But he could make logical guesses, based on what he had observed. Probably more accurately, he could also make assumptions based on what his gut told him. Add to it his years of experience, sitting up at night, fearing the dark.

He certainly wasn't the only kid in history ever to fear the Boogeyman. The legends and stories long predated him, as did Franny's news reports of disappearances. He would likely never know for sure, but he suspected that for most kids who had encountered the dark force hiding in a closet or under the bed, the meeting was short—he came and left, never to return.

But then there were the others, the lost ones, who he took away with them. Mostly children, based on Franny's records, but also adults. Tim didn't know how he chose his victims, or if it was purely a matter of who was convenient at any given time.

For whatever reason, he had chosen Rob Jensen, Tim's father. And Tim had witnessed his attack. Tim believed it was that—the fact that he had been a living witness to one of his predations—that had put him on the Boogeyman's list after that. He could probably have come for Tim at any time, and until his long sessions with Dr. Matheson, the boy had worried that every night would be the time. Now Tim thought the only reason the Boogeyman hadn't come for him was that he'd enjoyed Tim's terror so much. Why take him away when he had already made him fear the dark so much?

Somehow, the events of the last few days had changed the Boogeyman's priorities. Tim's mother's death—which perhaps the Boogeyman had foreseen, in some way—was the catalyst that drove Tim back home, back to where Franny was, back to where the secrets could be unveiled. Instead of being a compliant plaything, Tim became a threat. So the Boogeyman, trying to force Tim off his track, to terrify him back into submission, took those closest to Tim.

Which was encouraging, in a sick way. Because the Boogeyman wouldn't be worried if there wasn't something Tim could do to fight back.

Tim squeezed the familiar wooden handle of the bat, emboldened by the realization, and swung it.

But he didn't take aim at the Boogeyman—instead he smashed it into the black bird that dangled from the ceiling like it was some kind of miniature piñata. Plastic splinters flew everywhere—feathers and beak and feet—and the string that had suspended it snapped, coiled briefly around the bat, then released and dropped to the ground.

When Tim hit the bird, the Boogeyman reacted. Fragments flew from his shadowed form, like the shards of bird plastic, and vanished into the closet. The Boogeyman screamed, a sonic shockwave of a scream that buffeted Tim and Kate against the walls. *He can be hurt*, Tim realized with a grim smile. It was the best news he'd had all night.

Before Tim could even raise the bat again, however, the Boogeyman rearranged his shadow-stuff, and he was whole once again. He started toward Tim, intent on stopping him.

No one said it was going to be easy.

Tim lifted the bat and brought it down on the remains of the plastic bird once more, then a third time. Each time, the bird shattered into more pieces. And each time, the Boogeyman exploded a little more too, bits of him flying off and into the closet. The Boogeyman screamed twice, the sound like rusty railroad spikes being driven into Tim's ears, rattling his concentration.

"Stop it, Tim! Stop!" He caught a glimpse of Kate, huddled in the corner, hands clapped over her ears.

Tears ran down her face, and Tim thought there might have been blood trickling from between her fingers.

There was no stopping now, though. Too late for that. Tim wouldn't have been surprised to learn that his own ears were bleeding, his eardrums ruptured. He was hurting himself, sure, and maybe Kate too. But he was hurting the Boogeyman more. That, he couldn't give up on.

He turned his attention to the sparking, flashing nebula ball. In his mind's eye he pictured boyhood idol Roberto Clemente's swing, and he tried to emulate it. Pull back, release, follow through. The bat arced on a perfect plane and sliced through the nebula ball. For a split second Tim thought the bat had dematerialized, but then the ball shattered, glass spraying everywhere as if in slow motion.

The sonic blast of the Boogeyman's anguish shoved Tim with the force of a giant hand, slamming him into Kate. They both went down. As Tim pulled himself off her, he looked toward the Boogeyman. Sparks flew from him, lightning snapped as if from a storm cloud, like he had somehow internalized the nebula ball's electricity and was now releasing it himself.

Tim didn't know how long he could keep this up, or how well the Boogeyman could recover from the assault. The bat felt heavier now, his own breathing labored. It felt like each breath shredded his already raw lungs a little more. His legs protested when he tried to rise again, and the bat slipped from aching, cramped fingers, clattering on the floor.

But in the center of Tim's room, the Boogeyman reassembled himself yet again. The shadow-stuff that formed him must have been infinite, or nearly so. Tim figured he had better put an end to this fast, or he wouldn't be around for the finale.

He lunged for the bathrobe draped over the back of his chair. The Boogeyman charged toward him, as if trying to stop him before he could reach it. But Tim got it in both hands, dug his fingers into the terrycloth, and pulled with everything he had. He allowed himself a wicked smile—the Boogeyman wouldn't have tried so hard to keep him from this if it wasn't important.

The robe tore down the center seam.

The Boogeyman ripped apart too, right down the middle.

As he separated, a ferocious vacuum wind picked up, like that inside a pressurized airplane with a broken window. Shreds of the tattered Boogeyman were sucked into the closet. But so was everything else. The pieces of the plastic bird flew into it, the tiny glass shards of the nebula ball. Clothes, comics, books, a baseball glove and lamp from his bureau, the blinds from the window. Sheets from the bed took flight like massive wings and disappeared into the vortex. The bed itself started to stutter in that direction, as did Tim's desk and dresser.

The Boogeyman fought against the pull of the powerful wind. He stood with his feet far apart, his legs braced, his loose black clothing thundering, and tried to advance on Tim and Kate.

Kate had hooked an arm around a wall-mounted radiator and snagged Tim with her other hand. Their clothes flapped and fluttered, but she managed to hang on, to keep them from the gravitational force, the black hole inside Tim's closet that sucked all matter toward it.

The Boogeyman came forward a step, and then, struggling with Herculean effort, another one. Tim knew he didn't have the strength to fight back anymore—it was all he could do to withstand the suction, to keep holding on to Kate. If the Boogeyman reached them, they were done.

He watched as all the remnants of his childhood vanished into the closet, the wind picking up steam as if it were feeding on the energy of Tim's life. His nightstand took flight—

—and jolted by a sudden burst of inspiration, Tim snatched at it, leaning out, perilously close to breaking Kate's grasp—

—and he closed his hand around the drawer pull. The rest of the nightstand tumbled through the air, bouncing off the Boogeyman as it flipped and fell into the closet. All the drawer's contents took flight, following its path.

Except for one thing.

Tim closed his hand around the He-Man action figure. He heard the Boogeyman scream, even over the roar of the wind, as he raised his hand high. The plastic figure was aged and brittle. Tim felt it starting to crack in his grasp. He hurled it to the floor with every bit of strength he could manage, and it shattered there, not like an old and hardened action figure, but like blown glass, like fine china, into a million tiny pieces.

The Boogeyman's wail of pain sliced into Tim's ears. The room seemed to upend like a sinking ship, the open closet at the bottom, everything else emptying into it. Tim's boyhood bed dropped to the closet and squeezed through the opening, vanishing on the other side. Kate still maintained her grip on the radiator, though she dangled, the wind batting at her, trying to break her free.

She gave a little scream, and Tim thought she was losing her grip. He reached for her, to make sure she stayed put.

And in that second, he let go just long enough. He fell.

He saw the closet door waiting like the mouth of a starving beast, saw everything else in the room falling through it.

But Tim's chair was in his path, and he slammed against it, grabbed on.

The screws squealed as the incredible force tugged them from the wood, one by one. Tim saw the first give way completely and spiral down into the closet.

The Boogeyman clung to the floor, his shadowy claws digging furrows in the wood. He lunged at Tim, his grasping hand almost reaching the chair, but he rose too far off the floor, and the wind caught him.

His final scream echoing painfully, the Boogeyman

flew through the closet door. Tim's bureau squeezed through right after him, and the room was empty but for Tim, Kate, and the chair.

The chair had almost lost its moorings, bounced up and down on the wooden floor like an anxious tot.

And Tim was losing his grip, his sweaty fingers sliding off the wood . . .

Looking up, he saw Kate dangling above him, staring down, fear contorting her lovely face. The radiator had torn mostly free of the wall, and though she clung to it heroically, her weight added to the wind tugged at its last point of anchor.

It snapped, and Kate fell toward him.

Tim reached out to catch her, forced to release the chair to do it.

At that moment, the closet door slammed shut.

The room righted itself. Tim, Kate, and the broken radiator fell to the floor.

The incredible wind had gone quiet. Tim rose to his knees, bruised and bloody. A thin trail of blood trickled from Kate's nose and ears, her hair was an insane tangle, her clothes torn and disheveled.

Tim figured he must look worse.

Standing carefully, like a sailor taking his first step onto dry land after a year at sea, he walked to the closet. Held onto the knob for a second, listening. No sound issued from within. He twisted the knob, opened the door.

Inside, a wooden rod waited for hangers, an empty shelf above that. He reached past, tapped the back wall. Firm. Solid.

Just a closet.

Shutting the door again, Tim went back to Kate and offered her a hand. She took it, and he helped her to her feet. She leaned into him, holding his shoulders, and he wrapped an arm protectively around her.

"Don't be afraid of him, Kate," Tim told her. He had heard those words before, even said them himself, a time or two. The difference was, he was pretty sure he was right this time. "He can't come back if we're not afraid."

Kate's voice was tremulous, not as certain as Tim's. But she hadn't been through as much of it as he had, Tim knew. She didn't have all the information yet, had no way of knowing what it was they had just so narrowly survived. He would make sure that she did, he swore to himself, before the darkness came again. They had come through the dark night, even though so many others—Tim's dad, Uncle Mike, Jessica, Franny, all the lost ones over the years—had not.

Still, perhaps by beating the Boogeyman, this one time, he had avenged all of those heartrending losses in some small way. And by showing the Boogeyman that he *could* be defeated, maybe he'd made an even bigger difference.

"Okay," Kate said. Her tone was hushed, still fearful.

Tim glanced toward the window. The sky had lightened, the sun had just cleared the horizon. He released Kate and went to the window, opening it wide. It hadn't been washed in a very long time, and a layer of grime covered it, filtering the sun's rays.

But when he opened the window, pure, fresh morning sunlight flooded the room. Tim took it in, felt it splash across his cheeks and forehead like heavenly nectar. It was always night someplace—but then, that meant it was always morning someplace too.

Looking at him, even Kate managed a smile.

Epilogue

Shelby Stevenson could barely keep her sleepy eyes open. She lay in her bed, with Wooly the Lamb clutched in one hand, her blankets tucked tight around her. Her mother sat on the edge of her bed, and her weight tugged the blanket even more snugly there. Shelby liked the press of her mother on the bed, didn't want her to go. But they had finished tonight's storybook, and the rule was only one book each evening. Shelby knew her mom had work to do, dishes to wash, and she was tired.

But she didn't want her mother to leave.

Her mother knew that, knew all of Shelby's stalling routines. She opened the music box on the nightstand, and the ballerina rose up out of it, turning in her never-ending pirouette as the music tinkled.

"Since we have such a long drive tomorrow," Mom said, "I was going to pick you up early from school."

Shelby thought maybe Mom had said something earlier about them taking a long drive, but she couldn't remember the details. She yawned, pressing one of her fists against her mouth like she'd been taught. To keep the devil out, her mother had told her. She thought Mom had been teasing, but sometimes she got confused. Anyway, stuff like that scared her. "Where are we going?"

Her mother smoothed a few fine hairs away from Shelby's forehead. "Remember, honey, we're seeing that lady doctor. She's supposed to be real good with kids." Mom smiled and stood up. The bed shifted when she got off it, the covers suddenly looser. Shelby gripped the edge of the blanket and pulled it up to her chin. "She's going to help you," Mom said.

Stifling another yawn, Shelby replied. "Okay, Mom."

Her mother bent at the knees and the waist, leaned in, and kissed Shelby on the cheek. Shelby loved the feel of her mom's lips there, loved the scent of her, like fresh flowers in a meadow. But something was wrong tonight. Mom's smile didn't seem quite real—she was showing more teeth than she normally did, and her eyes didn't twinkle like when she was really happy.

She had been like that more and more lately, Shelby knew. She was afraid that maybe she was the cause of her mother's unhappiness. Mom tried to keep a smile on her face, and always had nice things to say. But she got tired so easily, these days, and there were more lines around her mouth and eyes than Shelby remembered ever seeing. Sometimes, when they thought Shelby couldn't hear them, she heard Mom and Dad talking about her, using the same serious voices as when they talked about paying the bills and grown-up stuff like that.

Mom started to reach for the lamp on Shelby's nightstand, and Shelby tensed, ready to remind her. But Mom caught her hand at the last minute, and just touched the shade, as if she had only been moving to adjust it. "Nighty night," she said.

"Nighty night," Shelby echoed. That was their routine, and she didn't like any variation from it.

"Don't let the bedbugs bite."

Mom turned and walked purposefully from the room, out into the hallway, leaving the door open a crack.

Alone now, Shelby snugged the covers tight to her chin, holding on with both hands. Her muscles were tense, balled up, her eyes wide open.

She thought she was safe. The light was on. Her mattresses were flat against the floor, so there was no space under the bed. Instead of having her clothes in a chest, they were arranged in small, careful piles, right up against the wall. The door to her closet was stored out in the garage, and a bright bulb burned inside it, making sure no shadows dwelt there. The overhead light was on, as was the lamp on the nightstand.

Beyond the circle of light, Shelby knew, lay a world of darkness.

But it couldn't touch her in here. . . .

About the Author

JEFF MARIOTTE is the author of more than twenty novels, including several set in the universes of *Buffy the Vampire Slayer*™ and *Angel*™, *Charmed*™, *Star Trek*®, and *Gene Roddenberry's Andromeda*™, the original horror novel *The Slab,* and the teen horror series *Witch Season,* as well as more comic books than he has time to count, some of which have been nominated for Bram Stoker and International Horror Guild awards. With his wife, Maryelizabeth Hart, and partner, Terry Gilman, he co-owns Mysterious Galaxy, a bookstore specializing in science fiction, fantasy, mystery, and horror. He lives on the Flying M Ranch in southeastern Arizona with his family and pets, in a home filled with books, music, toys, and other examples of American pop culture. More information than you would ever want to know about him is at www.jeffmariotte.com.

Not sure what to read next?

Visit Pocket Books online at
www.SimonSays.com

Reading suggestions for
you and your reading group
New release news
Author appearances
Online chats with your favorite writers
Special offers
And much, much more!

POCKET BOOKS
A Division of Simon & Schuster
A VIACOM COMPANY

POCKET
STAR BOOKS
A Division of Simon & Schuster
A VIACOM COMPANY

10421